UGLYVILLE

WRITTEN STUFF BY SAWNEY HATTON

Dead Size (A Novel)
Uglyville (A Novella)
Everyone Is a Moon (Short Stories)

EDITED STUFF BY SAWNEY HATTON

What Has Two Heads, Ten Eyes, and
Terrifying Table Manners? (An Anthology)

To Mom & Dad

UGLYVILLE

Published by
Dark Park Publishing

Cover design by
Milan Jovanovic

1st Ebook Edition: May 2015
1st Print Edition: August 2015

This Print Edition ISBN: 978-0-9886444-5-8

POLICE DEPARTMENT, COUNTY OF NASSAU, NEW YORK
EVIDENCE REPORT

Case Number: __3199__   Tag Number: __003199-05__

☒ Seized Pursuant to Search Warrant   Date: __5-5-86__

☐ Owner   ☐ Victim   ☐ Finder   ☒ Suspect

Name: __VERONA CASSIDY__   Phone: __N/A__

Address: __404 BIRCHWOOD CT.__

City: __MERRICK__   State: __NY__   Zip: __11566__

Booking Number: __NCP712976__

☐ Crime   ☐ Misdemeanor   ☒ Felony   ☐ Other

Details: __SEARCH & SEIZURE__

Description:
1. __diary, item #003199-05-1, from bedside table in susp bedrm__
2. __sneakers (mud), item #003199-05-2, from closet in susp bedrm__
3. __shoebox w/ photos (3), item #003199-05-(3-5), closet in susp bedrm__
4. __art & craft kit, item #03199-05-6, from desk in susp bedrm__
5. _____
6. _____
7. _____
8. _____
9. _____
10. _____

Recovered By: __DET. JEROME HAYES__   Badge Number: __2813__

Date: __5-5-86__   Time: __10:45 am__

Location: __404 BIRCHWOOD CT. MERRICK NY 11566__

Prepared By: __DET. JEROME HAYES__   Badge Number: __2813__

Date/Time Booked: __5-5-86 12:40 pm__   Approved By: __LT. BOB LUDEN__

Looking from a window above
It's like a story of love

—from the song "Only You"
by Yaz

FOREWORD
by Sawney Hatton

The passage of time and instances of even more sensational stories following it (like that of another Long Island native, Amy Fisher) have relegated the case of Verona Cassidy to the dustbin of history. Indeed, if one were to peruse the few newspaper articles covering the crime and its court proceedings in 1986-87, hers may seem just another incident of a teenage crush gone tragically wrong. This, however, truly does not do justice to Verona Cassidy's account.

I grew up in Merrick, New York, the same South Shore town Verona had hailed from ten years before me. I only became aware of her when researching a paper for my college criminology class on trends of youth-perpetrated felonies in my hometown. A Newsday item related the particulars of the crime, without disclosing the accused's name because of her age. It piqued my curiosity. With some sleuthing, I uncovered Verona's identity, but little else about her. She has stuck with me ever since.

Thanks to my recent success procuring the texts of both her personal journals—one written immediately prior to the commission of the crime and the other shortly after its jurisprudential outcome—the public can finally be privy to the workings of Verona's eccentric mind and the scope of her heinous deeds. Her thoughts transcribed verbatim in the pages herein may not wholly explain what compelled her to go to such extremes for love, yet they illuminate the degree of her dysfunction and delusion, indicators of a developing sociopathy.

While I attempted to seek out for this book any individuals involved or familiar with the decades-old case—family, friends, neighbors, police, attorneys—I found they were all either deceased, unlocatable, unable to remember much of interest, or unwilling to share it. As such, Verona's words must stand on their own, serving as the enduring testimony of a troubled girl with starry-eyed dreams, a broken moral compass, and a heart driven by fanciful romantic notions that ultimately shattered the lives of everyone she knew.

The Diary of Verona Cassidy*

*transcribed by Sawney Hatton
from original court facsimile

PRELUDE

My name is Verona Cassidy, I am 15 years old, and I am beautiful.

Glamorous beautiful. Movie star beautiful. Rita Hayworth beautiful.

Please don't think me conceited, all full of myself. I am only stating a fact. Beautiful is what I am. Who I am. My mom says I have wonderful genes. And I'm even prettier than her.

Make no mistake, it's not easy! Beauty takes a lot of work but it's so worth it. Being beautiful makes you look forward to each and every day. All those people who aren't beautiful, they admire you and envy you and imagine what it's like to be you. It makes you special.

Someday I will be up on the Silver Screen, larger than life, where people from all over the world can see me and adore me and want me. But only the handsomest of men can have me. I am after all special.

Starting now I shall document my journey to stardom.

Soon I will realize my destiny.

Then everybody will know how beautiful I am.

April 6, 1986

It's Sunday. I finished dusting the whole house so now I'm just lounging in my room writing this.

I dust the house once a week. It's one of my "jobs" here at the Cassidy homestead. It baffles me how, even though I get rid of all the dust every Sunday, the following weekend the same amount of it is on EVERYTHING again! I know we always bring in new dirt and fluff from outside or wherever, but come on. It's endless. It's ridiculous. I'm sure movie stars never dust their own homes. They had maids and servants. I guess I'm pretty much my mom's maid but I don't get paid for it. Instead I earn "privileges" like staying up later and decorating my room any way I choose.

My room's walls and ceiling are painted a deep shade of red, scarlet is what I call it but the can said it was something else I can't remember. And there's these gold clouds spread all around that I applied myself with a sponge last summer. Red and gold, the colors of passion and princesses.

I have an elegant rosewood canopy bed draped with white mosquito netting that used to belong to my Grammy, as did my vanity table (as a young woman Grammy was a champion cakewalker — that's a type of dance — in vaudeville). On the walls are framed photos and posters of all my idols and my beloveds.

On the right side, the Golden Age of leading men: Clark Gable, Humphrey Bogart, Gregory Peck, Cary Grant, Kirk Douglas, Gary Cooper, Burt Lancaster & Montgomery Clift in From Here to Eternity, Robert Mitchum, Victor Mature, Rock Hudson, and Tyrone Power (my vote for handsomest man in the movies)

On the left are the glamorous ladies of Classic Hollywood: Barbara Stanwyck, Marilyn Monroe, Rita Hayworth (from Gilda), Bette Davis, Betty Grable, Liz Taylor, Audrey Hepburn, Joan Crawford, Lana Turner (from Imitation of Life), Ingrid Bergman,

Lauren Bacall, and Grace Kelly (she became a real life princess!)

Every one is a legend. Every one is immortalized.

Someday I will be one of them!

April 7

I didn't get the part!!!

Last week I auditioned for the female lead role of Aldonza in our high school theater group's production of the musical "Man of La Mancha." I recited several of her lines and sang half of her theme song. I thought I nailed it. I KNOW I did.

But this morning I went to the callboard by the box office to see the posted cast list. I didn't get Aldonza. I got the Housekeeper. My character doesn't even have a proper name.

Lorraine York got my part instead. Again! She always gets the lead. Oh, she can act alright. She acts sweet as a pixie stick but she's really a cunning vampress. She's mesmerized our drama teacher Mr. Sardino. You can tell by the way he strokes his beard and stares at her and smiles when she's performing that he's got the hots for her. It's totally gross. And she's not even that good an actress, unless the role is a tree. She plays wooden well.

I couldn't help but cry when I got the news. I was weepy eyed all the way to my locker. To make matters worse, Ellen Goldfarb, Calhoun High's head cheerlessleader, calls me Pippi Longface because I have a few freckles.

"What's wrong Pippi Longface?" she said. "Find out you're an ugly boy instead of an ugly girl? Either way nobody's ever gonna love you."

Grrrr. She's such a b---h. And look who's talking ugly! She's always making herself up like a clown. All the so called popular girls in my school dress like cheesy Cyndi Lauper or Madonna wannabes. And here I am, bringing some classiness to the classroom and they laugh at me. Even the nerdy girls and goth girls act like I'm invisible. They know I'm not one of them and I never want to be.

Since it was a nice day today most of the other students went outside for lunch so I was able to get a table in the cafeteria all to myself. For a little while anyway.

Howie Gutermuth decides it was the perfect opportunity to ask me out again. I soundly rejected him of course. Howie is in most of my classes (except Biology and Art) and always tries to sit closest to me if the seating isn't assigned alphabetically. He's chubby, his hair is so greasy it shines, and he has these double humped lips that look too big for his face. He also stutters when he's nervous, which is most of the time.

"I'd never date you in a zillion years," I told him.

"How ab-b-bout a z-z-zillion and one?" he answered.

That's about as cute as Howie got.

I got home from school at 3. My mother wouldn't be back from work until 7 at the earliest, sometimes as late as midnight. I ate the last of the leftover meatloaf and caught the second half of The Sandpiper on TV, starring real life husband & wife Richard Burton & Liz Taylor. Despite the marvelous actors it wasn't especially good. I then went up to my room and after writing all this I'm figuring I should just go to bed early.

Today was a dreadful day.

April 8

Since yesterday was such a disaster, to make myself feel better I decided today I'd make myself up like one of my idols. I picked Veronica Lake, putting on deep red lipstick, dark eyebrows, curled eyelashes, a hint of shadow, and a lock of my wavy strawberry blonde hair falling over my face. (This is called a peek-a-boo bang.)

I smiled in my mirror. Veronica smiled back.

I put on my lacy satin dress. By the time I got downstairs my mother was ready to go to work. Her blouse as usual was unbuttoned enough to advertise her assets. She was rummaging through her purse.

I asked her if she had misplaced something. She said she lost a phone number jotted on a Fortunoff receipt. She found it on a Macy's receipt. She frequently confuses department stores like that. She's forgetful a lot too, though mostly about small stuff like where she puts things. I wonder if the pills she takes for her moodiness are affecting her brain.

She began medicating herself after she divorced my father. I was 9. We kept our three bedroom house in Merrick and he moved into an apartment somewhere on the east side of Manhattan. This period of my life was most unpleasant. Before my father left there was a lot of yelling and slamming of doors and moments of tense silence while they stewed over whatever they had been yelling about. I was miserable. I even tried to end it all, slashing my wrist with a dinner knife.

Obviously I failed. It didn't even leave a scar.

Before my mother left for her job (she's a realtor) she said I looked nice and asked me what the occasion was.

"It's a Tuesday" I replied.

She laughed at that and promised me we'd have a Girls Night Out sometime next week. Which won't happen. It never does.

As soon as I arrived at school Howie greets me at my locker. I was much sweeter to him today because I wanted to copy his Social Studies homework and he also said I looked great. I let my dress slide off my shoulder a moment so he could see my bra strap. I even called him "darling." I can tell he loves that.

Yes I'm a tease. But all the most beautiful women are.

In art class I'm painting a movie poster featuring yours truly in my future Hollywood debut. I'm leaning back on a divan in a flowing sky blue gown, looking suitably ravishing and tormented, and on the bottom is written VERONA CASSIDY IN THE WOMAN WITH THE EMERALD EYES. It's turning out splendid. When it's finished I'll hang it over my bed, replacing the picture of Snow White my parents bought me at Disneyland an ice age ago.

April 11

I haven't written anything here the last couple of days because there wasn't much to write about. School the usual, life the usual. In the movies they cut out the boring parts of the story, the ones where the characters are just sleeping or driving around or shopping for groceries. Hence I'm only going to record the interesting or entertaining bits of my life so I don't bore my fans reading this in the future.

Today Ellen Goldfarb hurt herself in cheerleading practice, which seemed to upset a lot of people who aren't me. She twisted her ankle (it should have been her neck!) and will have to miss a few precious football games. I saw her crying about it in the hall outside the nurse's office, like it was the worst thing that ever could happen to her. I've missed EVERY football game our school's ever had and it hasn't bothered me a whit.

I told her that I hope it heals OK and she doesn't walk funny for the rest of her life.

That's not true of course. I hope she walks like the Hunchback forever.

This morning Howie got sent to the Principal's office for sassing some jock who was being a jerk to him and they got into a fight and both of them were given detention after school. Howie told me all about it at lunch. The only thing I really remember was his busted bottom lip, still swollen and scabbed over looking like a butchered caterpillar. It wasn't the first one he'd gotten. He couldn't smile lest it start bleeding again, which was fine by me. He has the goofiest smile.

What else? My mother came home late from work again so I made myself a Le Menu microwave dinner and watched TV. When she got in she was really tipsy and her blouse was open more than usual. Which was not unusual for her. Out hunting for a new husband no doubt, for another father to raise me. As if one wasn't bad enough.

Speaking of, I'll be spending this weekend at my father's house. That should be fun. NOT

April 12

It's Saturday night and I'm at my father's, avoiding my father. God he's such a boor!

My mother dropped me off here shortly before noon. She drives only Volvos, which ever since Sex Ed reminds me of the word "vulva." Sometimes I call it that just to be funny and make my mom laugh. I can't wait to learn how to drive so I can ask her to borrow her vulva.

Anyway, I went into my father's house (I have my own key) and call out for him. He doesn't answer so I go searching for him.

My dad's new house is in Westchester, north of the city. It's built at the top of a hillside and the 2nd floor juts out over the trees and has these high ceilings and entire walls made up of windows. It has an awesome view of the Hudson Valley. The home must be worth millions, which my father can well afford being an enter-tainment lawyer for a major record label.

The house has lots of rooms and I checked every one for my father. Judging by all the empty wine bottles and glasses everywhere, I guessed he must have had some big soirée last night. Somebody left their pantyhose on the lamp in his bedroom. The air still smelled like expensive perfume. Some vile porno video was still playing on the VCR. I shut it off.

I finally find my father outside on the bottom of the pool. There's no water in it. Dad's not much of a swimmer but he likes the idea of owning a house with a pool and throws the occasional pool party in the summer for his rich friends. He was just lying there in a chaise at the deep end, wrapped up in his red robe and holding an empty margarita glass sideways. He looked dead.

"Dad!" I yelled.

He jolted awake and squinted up at me.

"Hey rosebud. Here already?"

No matter how much you reminded my father what time I was coming over, he always acted surprised by my arrival. Like he forgot to pencil me into his calendar.

This wasn't even the worst part of the day. Once my father regained some level of consciousness he decided he wanted to hang out with me instead of gabbing on the phone like he usually does the whole time I'm here. So I'm watching the Bette Davis classic Now, Voyager on cable. At the end Bette says the famous line to her lover Paul Henreid, "Don't let's ask for the moon. We have the stars." Which means enjoy what you have and don't pine over what you don't. (I'll take the stars AND the moon, thank you!)

Anyway, dad plops down next to me on the sofa. He looks tanned and terrible.

"What are you watching?" he asks.

I tell him.

He nods, calling Bette Davis the "one with the eyes." He sings a few lines of the song. It's a good song that sounds like a man's dying breaths when sung by my father.

Then he asks me, I kid you not, "When did you get boobs?"

I was speechless. I was mortified. I stormed into the guest bedroom which is my room when I'm visiting. Then I started writing this.

I can hear my father somewhere in the house talking loudly on his phone. I wonder if he will ever shut up.

April 13

I'm back home now. Mom picked me up at 6 from my father's.

This morning dad & I managed to have something close to a pleasant breakfast together. He didn't mention my chest and asked me how school was going, but we didn't talk about much else. We never have much to talk about. We don't really understand each other nor have anything in common. We may as well be from entirely different families. Or species — I live up in the trees, he lives underground.

On the ride home mom asked me if I had fun. I shrugged. She didn't ask me how dad was. She never does.

When we got in she says she bought me something special from the mall, which turned out to be this denim handbag covered in pink rhinestones shaped like hearts. She asks me if I liked it.

"It's not really my style" I tell her, because it really isn't. I only carry chic clutches.

"But it's very popular with girls your age," she says.

I say "Then give it to one of them."

My mother calls me ungrateful, says fine she'll return it, and doesn't speak another word to me the rest of the night. God she can be so childish sometimes.

April 14

O my heart is pounding like a jack-hammer! I'm too excited not to write this down right this instant. If I'm late for school so be it.

I'm in love!!!

I was almost done getting ready when I glanced out my window and saw him. I couldn't take my eyes away, I refused to even blink!

He has an impressive brawny physique and feathery raven hair and a chiseled broody face like Marlon Brando's in A Streetcar Named Desire. The kind of man they don't make anymore, as Grammy would say. He wore a white T-shirt, blue jeans and workboots, and bulky gray gloves. He strode up to my house, grabbed the trashcan from the curb with one strong arm and emptied it into the truck. He then removed his gloves, lit a cigarette and took a drag, then hopped onto the footstep on back of the truck and gallantly rode it up the street around the corner and out of my sight.

My garbageman is dreamy beyond my most fantastic dreams! I don't think I will ever want another as much as him

[[BREAK]]

In English class I drew a **picture of my garbageman**[*] which I have clipped here

> [*]ITEM CATALOGED 05/05/1986
> NASSAU COUNTY P.D. CASE # 003199
> EVIDENCE LOG # 003199-05-1a

After I finished it I swear I saw his big yellow truck parked outside my classroom window. Then when I looked next to me there he was in a top hat and tails sitting at the desk beside mine!

"Hey there beautiful" he crooned, smiling his perfect smile. "How about we get out of here?"

I nodded. He extended his hand and I took it. We rose from our seats and he led me out of the classroom, through the hallway, and into the gym. I was now magically dressed in a luxurious white gown and glittery diamond jewelry. I looked fabulous! Ballroom music swelled around us and I waltzed with him up and down the bleachers and across the polished wood floors, just like Fred Astaire & Ginger Rogers.

Then Ellen Goldfarb or one of her b---h friends hit me in the head with a dodge-ball.

"Stay awake Pippi" Ellen said. She's still hobbling around on crutches because of her ankle. Why was she even in gym class today? Why doesn't somebody just shoot her and put her out of my misery?

April 16

I admit it, I'm obsessed.

All day today and all day yesterday all I could think about was my ~~garbage~~ gorgeousman. His face appears in the cars driving by, up in the clouds, even in my food!

How ever did you get into my baked ziti, my love?

He is always beckoning me, begging me to be with him. Tormenting me with those hypnotic eyes of his. It's maddening how much I want him. How much I need him. There is nothing so devastating as the pain between two lovers who have not yet joined but are destined to be together! I know we are!

Sometimes, dear fans, you have to nudge Fate along. So I composed a love letter to him on my mom's fancy stationery.

Here is what I wrote:

Dear Handsome Garbageman,

I am your Mystery Admirer. I am beautiful, available and willing. I'd love to make your acquaintance... and more.

Meet me in the gazebo at Briarwood Park at 7 PM tonight. I promise you won't be disappointed!

Your Damsel in a Dress,
V

I had to rewrite it 11 times. My words, my punctuation, my penmanship had to be flawless. I only wish I knew his name so I could address him properly, but I am sure he will know it is for him.

I neatly folded the letter and slid it into the envelope. I didn't know what to write on the outside so I put on some ruby red lipstick and kissed the flap, leaving my mark, my message screaming "These lips yearn for yours!"

Our block's trash pick-up days are Mondays & Thursdays. I saw my gorgeousman on Monday and I hope he works both days. I'm praying he does! If I have to wait until next Monday I think my heart will explode!!!

I'm certain I won't be able to sleep tonight. Tomorrow morning cannot arrive quick enough!

April 17

God must be laughing at me. My plan didn't turn out quite the way I expected it to.

This morning before the crack of dawn I stuck my love letter, which I spritzed with Coco Chanel perfume, into the handle of our trashcan set out on the curb. Then I sat at my bedroom window and waited for Gorgeousman to show up at my house and find it.

When I spotted the garbage truck rolling up my block, I noticed there were 2 men picking up the trashcans and dumping them into the truck. One was Gorgeousman! But to my horror I realized he was taking trashcans from the wrong side of the street. Some fat bald guy was doing my side, which meant he would find my letter!

I panicked. It was too late to run down and retrieve the letter, they were now only one house away from mine. So I opened my window and poked my head out. On our roof by my window was this cute

Siamese kitten ornament that my father had put there when I was little. I leaned out and grabbed it.

I am so not the athletic type. I don't play sports other than those I'm forced to take part in gym class. Nor do I ever watch sports. I know practically nothing about them. So when I threw the ceramic cat it was by sheer luck and mental will that it hit its target: the Fat Bald Guy's head.

Fat Bald Guy grunted and rubbed his forehead. It was bleeding. Gorgeousman went to him, probably asked him if he was OK. Fat Bald Guy made some theatrical gestures, no doubt explaining what had just happened. Gorgeousman picked up my broken cat from the street then looked all around. He even looked straight up at my window, but I ducked out of sight behind my curtains just in time.

A moment later I braved peeking out the window again. Fat Bald Guy now had a handkerchief pressed to his brow and was climbing into the passengers seat of the truck. Gorgeousman chucked the cat pieces into the truck's butt and walked over to my trashcan. He was going to find my letter!

Not.

Gorgeousman flipped the lid off and carried the trashcan over and emptied it into the truck. My love letter fell into the gutter by his feet. He didn't see it! He hopped back onto the back of the truck, slapped it like a horse's rump and off they drove around the corner.

I was terribly dismayed, dear fans. But I wasn't about to abandon hope yet!

I dashed outside in my silk pjs and fuzzy slippers, snatched the letter from the ground and ran up my street as fast as I could. I feared my house might have been the last one on their route but fortunately they still had Solsbury Lane to do.

I didn't want Gorgeousman to spot me so I raced into Mr. & Mrs. Vogler's back-yard. From there I cut through several other yards, leaping fences, dodging children's playsets, and trampling flower and vegetable gardens. When I saw I had gotten well enough ahead of the truck I darted out to the trashcans in front of whoever's house it was. I again placed my letter on top of one then went and crouched down behind some bushes. I lost a slipper on the way but it was too late to fetch it.

I watched with bated breath as Gorgeousman approached the trashcans. Before he grabs them he sees the envelope and picks it up. He examines it a while then opens it. I watch his face as he reads my words written for him. He glances all around, then slides the letter back in the envelope, folds it up and tucks it into his jeans pocket.

I would have shouted with glee if I hadn't still been hiding. Instead I watched him as he continued collecting garbage from the rest of the street.

Then I heard a woman's voice say "Pardon me young lady."

I looked up from the bushes and standing above me on the stoop was a middle-aged woman in a blue robe. I've seen her before around the neighborhood walking her poodle but I don't know her name.

"What do you think you're doing?" she asked me.

"Nothing" I said while I crept out of the bushes.

"Well, you look like you're up to something," says the woman.

I did feel a bit silly there and tried to concoct a believable excuse for why I was hanging out in her shrubs.

"I lost my slipper," I said. "Oh there it is!"

I ran over to the middle of the lawn and recovered it.

"How on earth did it get there?"

I only answered "thank you" and rushed home to get ready for school.

Hooray! Gorgeousman got my message! Now all I have to do is wait until tonight. Arrrgh. Waiting for your destiny to be fulfilled is such torture!

[[BREAK]]

God must hate me.

So I managed to get through the whole day at school without going stark raving mad from anticipation.

I got home by 2:30 and spent the next few hours making myself as ravishing as possible. I made up my face to capture the sensuous elegance of Lauren Bacall. I did up my hair in a french pleat like Audrey Hepburn in Breakfast At Tiffany's. I put on my strapless sparkly white ruffled dress that looks much like the one Rita Hayworth wore in The Lady From Shanghai. Lastly I slipped on a pair of white elbow length gloves and draped a vintage fox fur wrap (which had belonged to Grammy) over my shoulders.

I was stunning!

Gorgeousman will not be able to resist me!

I arrived at Briarwood Park a quarter before 7 and sat on the bench inside the gazebo. It wasn't as nice as I thought it would be. The paint was peeling off and there was a lot of graffiti, some of it quite crude. But I decided none of this really mattered. He was coming to see me and I could outshine even the filthiest pigsty!

7 o'clock came and passed. As did 7:15, 7:30, 8 o'clock. And still I waited. Hoping. Praying. Please Please Please

And then, just when I was convinced my prayers were going to go unanswered, a man's voice behind me said "Hi"

I turned around, ready to meet my Gorgeousman.

And there instead was Howie Gutermuth.

"What do you want Howie?" I'm sure I must have scowled at him.

He said "n-nothin'. I just saw you s-s-sitting here. Thought I'd say hello."

I said hello back and told him to go away.

He doesn't go of course. He tells me I look great. Like a movie star. (Which I now admit was a rather nice thing to say, but I wasn't in the mood for his niceness at that moment.) Then he asks me what I was doing there.

"I'm meeting someone" I answer. Not that it was any of his business.

"How long have you been waiting for?"

I told him only a few minutes.

He tells me it's been closer to an hour.

I was beyond outraged! I accused him of following me.

He said no he wasn't, explained how he had passed me on the way to the comic book store and on his way home saw I was still there.

"My date's running late but he'll be here very soon," I told him, hoping he would take the hint.

"What time was he supposed to meet you?" Howie asked.

7, I said.

Howie unhelpfully points out Gorgeous-man is way late.

I say I'm sure he has a good reason. Howie speculates he might have gotten lost. Then he suggests he might've blown me off because he wasn't that into me.

"Leave me alone" I snarled at Howie, giving him my best glare of wrath.

"Not that I b-b-believe that," Howie sputtered. "Who wouldn't be totally into you? He'd have to be a total loser n-not to be." Howie offered to hang out with me until Gorgeousman showed up, and if Gorgeousman didn't Howie could walk me home.

Yeah right, like that was ever going to happen.

I turned my back to him and said "Leave. Me. Alone."

Howie finally stopped pestering me. "Hope your date happens," he said and walked away.

I stayed another 45 minutes there in that rotting gazebo, read every word of graffiti a hundred times each, every T.C. + E.M. and Pete & Lania 4eva and Jason K Was Here and Jesus Is Lord and the most obscene phrases an immature boy can think of.

Gorgeousman never came.

I'm home now. I wept for a while into Flynn (my teddybear I've had since I was a toddler) then started writing this.

My fated love failed to appear at the appointed time of our introduction. But the question was, Why? Surely he must have been curious to lay eyes on the one who held the key to his heart.

Maybe he got sick or his car broke down. Perhaps he had a prior commitment that evening he couldn't get out of. After all, I never confirmed our plans with him. But wouldn't he have contacted me somehow if he couldn't make our date?

Or perhaps he already has a girlfriend. Or a wife. That would be so unfair!

Could he have thought it was a joke? That someone was cruelly mocking him?

O no, my darling, you are not the butt of some silly prank. My love is true and I'll prove it to you! You will see that my love is real. That I am real. That we are meant to be together.

Somehow...

April 18

I was so despondent I almost skipped school today. Luckily I didn't.

Instead of devising a means to ensnare my love, I dwelt on all the ways he would never be mine. Thus I spent most of the day moping through the halls and sulking in my classes. I paid zero attention to my teachers. I bumped into people. I must've gone to the bathroom a dozen times to cry in the stalls. I hated my life.

It was a rough day.

As soon as the dismissal bell rang I began walking home. All I wanted to do was lock myself in my room and veg. I considered pinching some of my mom's happy pills.

As usual I exited out the doors by the gym and cut through the field. The football team was practicing, as was the cheerleading squad. Gimpy Ellen Goldfarb sat on the bottom bench of the bleachers, acting like an army drill sergeant, barking directions at the other girls, telling them to kick higher! jump higher!

I tried to ignore them, until I noticed the football team had stopped playing. Every boy was staring at the cheerleaders, watching their boobies bounce with every jump, their skirts lift with every kick. Leering at them like starved wolves.

I smiled. I now know what I have to do.

April 21

I woke up this morning before the sun rose and wrote a new message for Gorgeousman. I was feeling good about myself. I spent the entire weekend exercising like crazy doing push-ups & sit-ups & jumping jacks, and not eating anything but carrots and celery. I was ready for him.

Was he ready for me??

I took the message to our trashcan out front. Because it was breezy out I taped it to the lid. The outside flap said GARBAGEMAN PLEASE READ. I returned upstairs and staked my place at my window.

I was awfully nervous but incredibly excited. I thought he better be working my side of the street today. I don't know if I could summon the courage to do this again!

I saw the big yellow truck turn onto my street. Gorgeousman was taking cans from my side. Hooray! I watched him head up the block, waited for him to find my message. He reached my house and swaggered toward my trashcan. He stopped at it, looking down at the top. Then he peeled my note from the lid. He unfolded it and read what I had written for him.

LOOK UP LOVER it said.

He did, and there I was in all my gloriousness.

I stood before my window, nude from the waist up. I arched my back and slid my fingers through my hair, making my bosom heave. I could see his sun-lit face squinting up at me, his eyes lingering over my body. Watching me, wanting me. When I thought his interest had been peaked enough, I winked at him and stepped away from the screen. My show lasted only a few seconds but it felt like a wondrous eternity, a timeless moment shared only between him & me.

At the very bottom of the message I designated the same time and place to meet tonight. I have no doubts he will come. I have offered myself to him completely — a virgin goddess willing to be thrown into the molten hot volcano. How could any man refuse that?

[[BREAK]]

I went. I waited. He never came.

I hate hate hate hate HATE my life.

[[BREAK]]

Oh my god!!! I think I'm going to have a heart attack!

I was much too melancholy to sleep so I went downstairs to watch TV. Written on the Wind starring Rock Hudson & Lauren Bacall & Robert Stack was on. It's about two best friends who fall in love with the same woman. It's a great movie, but tonight it made me sort of jealous. Here are 2 men both infatuated with one girl and I can't even rouse the attentions of a single man. What's wrong with me?

Dear fans, sometimes Destiny works in mysterious ways.

My mother got home later than usual, after midnight. As soon as she stepped through the door I could tell she was drunk, all giggly and slurring and dropping her keys. I realized she was talking to somebody. A man. And she was leading him through the house toward the den where I lay. Mom doesn't typically bring her boyfriends home unless she thinks they're "special." I was in no mood to be introduced to her Stud of the Month. Desperate to avoid them, I sprang from the floor and raced from the room.

As I was going through the kitchen and they were heading through the dining room, I glimpsed my mom's date and stopped dead in my tracks.

It was Gorgeousman!

"Hey V!" my mom called out. "I want you to meet someone."

I think I said something but I don't remember what it was.

"This is Rick. Rick, this is my daughter Verona."

Rick. His name is Rick.

"Hi there kiddo" he said in a voice smooth and rich as cream.

Rick wore a black sports jacket and black loafers and a half unbuttoned blue button-down shirt tucked into black Z Cavariccis. A gold chain glistened upon his bared chest. His dark hair was slicked back and shiny under the dining room light. He was handsomer than ever, looking like a young Tony Curtis.

He smiled at me — the no makeup, messy hair, wrinkled pajamas me.

"Hi" I said, my mouth hanging open like a retard.

"Are you OK honey? You don't look so well," my mom said.

I bolted for the stairs and rocketed up to my room. I slammed the door shut behind me and grabbed my teddybear Flynn from my bed and bashed him against the headboard again & again & again until his stuffing starting popping out. Then I hugged him for a long while. The poor guy had lost an eye.

A tempest of powerful emotions is sweeping through me. I can hardly breathe. Gorgeousman — Rick — is here, in my house, right now! I feel exhilarated, embarrassed and confused. He spoke to me, smiled at me, gazed upon me. But he didn't act like he recognized me at all. Maybe he was only being coy around my mother.

He was dating my mother!!!

I first thought this was terrible, a terrifying nightmare come true. He was meant for me! This was not happening!

Then I thought, yes this _is_ happening, but for a reason.

Destiny was not thwarting our love by giving Rick to my mom. Rather she was the means it was using to bring him to me! O Destiny, thou art clever!

[[BREAK]]

I'm back. I snuck downstairs to spy on Rick & my mom. I squatted on the bottom step and peered over the railing into the living room. They were sitting together on the couch, their faces way too close to each other. They were talking and laughing.

"You smell boozy" Rick said.

Then my mom says "Tell me how I taste."

55

And then they kissed!

"MOM!!!" I shouted, retreating a few steps up the stairs.

"What V?" my mom answered.

"I'm sick! I threw up!"

"S--t" I heard my mom mutter. "I'll be up in a minute hon!"

I ran back into my room, slipped under the blankets and put on my best ailing expression and waited. A few minutes later I heard the squeak of the front storm door. I dashed to the window.

My mother walked Rick to his cherry red Ford Mustang parked outside under the streetlamp. They kissed goodbye for a long time while I watched helplessly, grinding my teeth. Then Rick got into his car, started it, and roared down my block.

As upset as I was, I knew I couldn't jeopardize the grand plan Destiny had for Rick & me. I returned to my bed and fluttered my eyes and groaned. It was a magnificent performance.

My mom came in and sat down beside me on the bed. She took my temperature.

"You don't have a fever," she said.

I told her it could've been something I ate and that I was feeling better after I barfed. She said that's good but if I was still feeling icky tomorrow I should stay home from school.

My mom headed for the door and told me to get a good night's rest.

"How'd you meet Rick?" I asked her.

"At Flappy's" she answered. Flappy's is this sleazy bar in Bellmore.

"So you were drunk" I said.

"As a matter of fact I wasn't at all. I ordered a drink. Which I spilled. Rick came over and bought me another."

That was nice of him, I said. I asked if she intended to see him again.

Wednesday night, she answered.

"What are you going to do?"

Mom asks me what's with the twenty questions? I tell her I'm just interested in her welfare. She looked touched by that.

Mom says Rick's going to take her out to some fancy shmancy restaurant.

I feigned being impressed but I was fighting off a sneer. I should be the one going to a fancy shmancy restaurant with him!

Patience, Verona. Good things come to those who deserve them.

"Rick's an awesome guy," my mother says. "He's great looking, funny, a gentleman. He's our garbageman, y'know."

Oh really?

"You'd think he would stink a little from his work," mom said, "like that guy I was seeing from the fish market. But he doesn't at all. He must be really clean."

Too clean for you, mother.

"His job pays really well too," she continued. "I tell you V, he may be the one."

I say "I thought that guy you dated last summer — Ben — wasn't he supposed to be the one?"

Ben, she tells me, was married, and mom's nobody's #2.

Mom switched off my light, said sweet dreams and left my room.

I know I'll dream tonight, though I'm not sure how sweet they'll be.

April 22

I decided to go to school today, though my mind was scarcely there. I focused on how I was going to tempt Rick away from my mother. For most of the day I came up with no sensible ideas and this distressed me. If Rick was meant for me, shouldn't winning his heart be easier? I'm so not the type who likes a challenge. I just wanted him to be mine already.

But whatever I have to do I'll do. Just let me know what that is, Universe!

In my 3rd period English class, while Mr. Huston was rambling on about Jane Eyre, I imagined Rick & my mother making nooky right there behind him on the teacher's desk, which did not improve my foul mood in the least. Then Mr. Huston, who's never before made me answer a question I hadn't raised my hand for, decides today would be a jolly good day to do so.

"Miss Cassidy" he says to me, "What do you suppose Jane's feelings were regarding Miss Ingram?"

I answer "She likely thought she was a whore." A few of the other students snickered at this.

"And what makes you think that?" Mr. Huston asks.

"Any girl who steals away someone else's man is a whore." I thought this was a very logical argument.

"But Mr. Rochester is not Jane's lover," Mr. Huston says.

To which I say "Not yet."

Then Ellen Goldfarb the Gimp barks "Freak!" from the back of the room and everybody laughs. Everybody but me. I didn't care. I had far more important stuff to fret about.

After lunch I found Howie Gutermuth prying books out of his locker. He not only has his textbooks and notebooks in there, but tons of comic books and snack foods and all these odd toys I don't recognize. It's a mess. But that's Howie.

Howie does have one thing going for him. He can drive.

Today he was wearing one of his velour shirts, a maroon one with a tan W across the chest. It was pretty hideous but I bet Howie thought it made him look like a superhero.

I sashayed up beside him and said "Super shirt."

He dropped some of his books. I knelt down to pick them up for him, knowing he could see down my blouse just a little. Just enough.

"Thanks" he said. "It's v-v-velour."

I stroked the shirt, running my finger-tips up and down Howie's arm. I could feel him shiver at my touch. "It's like velvet," I told him. "I love it."

Howie gulped. His lips trembled. He was breathing harder. I knew he ~~wouldn't~~ couldn't refuse me.

"You have a driver's license, don't you?" I asked him.

He said he has a learner's permit.

I inquired if he had a car.

He told me his dad lets him borrow his if he isn't using it.

"How about you take me out for a ride tomorrow night?" I suggested.

For a moment I thought the boy's tongue had skipped town. Then he said "You mean, like on a d-d-date?"

Oh god no. But I didn't want to crush his hopes. I needed him.

"Let's call it a trial run," I said, batting my eyes.

Howie of course agreed.

Now I only have to figure out how to thwart my mom & Rick's rendezvous tomorrow night. I'm sure I'll come up with something bold and brilliant. I am very smart. Us beautiful women have to be. Beauty without brains will just end up getting a girl lost.

Mark my words, dear fans, I WILL find my way to Rick's heart!

April 23

So my idea may not have been brilliant but it was bold. Most important, I think it succeeded.

My mother squeezed herself into her sluttiest outfit and smeared her face with vibrant shades of trashy. I found her in the bathroom redoing her hair in the mirror for probably the millionth time. You can only brush and spray and crimp your hair so much, it's not going to get any bigger or curlier or stiffer. But mom kept trying.

"I'm going to the library," I told her.

"Studying?" she asked.

"No. Burning it down." She didn't laugh. I thought it was funny.

"Meeting Trish there?"

I didn't respond. I haven't been friends with Tricia Weinstein since our junior high prom when she stranded me there to go drink wine coolers with Jason Krauss. She does drugs now and plays hooky a lot. My mother obviously forgot this.

Mom asks me if I needed a ride. I said I could walk.

"OK sweetie" she says. "Take $10 from my purse for dinner."

I did that and also took her travel box of condoms. Then I left the house.

Howie was parked outside in his dad's navy blue Corolla a few houses down from mine. He dressed spiffy for our mission — black shoes and slacks, a purple sateen shirt, and a white blazer. He moussed his hair into a wave. He looked all ready to go disco dancing, a decade too late.

I didn't pay much attention to him. As soon as I got into the car my eyes were trained on my house. I couldn't miss my chance.

"I g-g-gotta g-get the car back by midnight," Howie said.

I told him that's fine.

Then he says "After we're done with this maybe we can go for some pizza?"

Oh god Howie, give it a rest! I thought.

Thankfully right then Rick's Mustang pulled up to my house and turned into my driveway behind our Volvo. He honked his horn and got out. My mother exited the house, locking the door behind her. She looked barely able to breathe in that skin-tight black dress of hers. It made her walk weird too. Or maybe that was because of the stilettos. She looked like one of those robotic women in that Robert Palmer music video.

Mom strutted up to Rick. He kissed her, a quick peck on her glossy red lips, which infuriated me. Then he opened the passenger door for her. She shimmied into the seat. Rick circled back around his car and hopped behind the wheel and drove off away from us.

"Don't lose them" I warned Howie.

"I won't" he promised me.

We followed them. Howie did a fine job keeping us at a discreet distance. They wound up at some Italian restaurant in Bay Shore. It didn't look all that fancy to me. Maybe Rick wasn't too serious about my mom.

We parked across the street where we had a clear view of them eating at a table by the window. They kept staring at each other while they talked. Sometimes my mom laughed. I tried to read their lips but I couldn't make out what they were saying but I'm pretty sure mom said my name a few times. I didn't like that she was speaking about me to him, even if it was probably all nice things.

I was concentrating so hard on them that I didn't notice how quiet it was in the car until Howie got bored and began drumming his fingers on the steering wheel.

I told him to please stop.

He did. Then he started squirming, as if his seat was poking him in different spots. And he sighed a lot.

I ignored him.

Then he said "I know you're worried about your mom and everything b-b-but this guy seems pretty normal." I'd told Howie I feared Rick was a homicidal maniac who quenched his bloodlust on lonely divorcees. He said Rick doesn't look like a psycho.

"They never do" I answered. "Now hush."

Howie sat there for an entire five more seconds before he interrupted my stake-out yet again. He announced he was hungry and was running over to the Taco Hut on the corner. He asked me if I wanted anything.

I turned toward him and said "Don't go. What if they leave?"

"They're still eating," he observed.

"But what if they decide not to finish their meals and he lures my mom to his lair while you're gone?" I said. "Something awful might happen while I'm stuck here waiting for you to get back."

"Taco Hut's right there," he pointed. "I won't be long at all. I'll b-be able to see you the whole time."

I reached over and put my hand on his thigh and gazed into his eyes pleadingly. "Please stay Howie. We'll go to the diner after this is done, OK?"

Howie agreed to this. He fished a tin of mints from his coat pocket and munched on them.

45 minutes later Rick & my mother paid for their meals and left the restaurant. We tailed them for about 20 minutes when Rick pulled up outside a brick apartment building in East Meadow. Howie coasted his car in front of the building next door.

Rick & my mom got out of the Mustang and he escorted her by the hand to the main entrance. They went in.

"You were right" Howie said. "He d-did lure her to his lair."

This was not good. Knowing my mother, she would seduce Rick within mere minutes. She'd have her lusty way with him, soiling him, tainting him.

Howie echoed my thoughts. "Probably gonna g-g-get bizzeee," he said.

I scowled at him. But he was right. I had to act fast!

I got out of the car and scanned the rows of apartment windows. I needed to find which one was Rick's. After a couple of minutes a light came on inside a 2nd floor apartment. I figured that was it. My assumption was proven correct when Rick stepped up to the window and drew the blinds.

"Guess the show's over," Howie said. "Unless you g-g-got X-ray glasses."

I panicked. It wouldn't take my mother long to take advantage of Rick's manly weaknesses. I pondered. What could I do?

"We're not g-g-gonna wait for them to come out?" Howie asked me. "They could be up there all night."

No! I couldn't allow that!

My mother is home! Be right back

[[BREAK]]

I'm back. Everything worked out splendid!

In my desperation to terminate their date, I skimmed the area all around me. What could I do from out there? That's when I spotted the flashing red light inside Rick's Mustang which gave me an idea. I found a chunk of concrete by the side-walk. I hefted it over to Rick's car and hurled it with all my might. It shattered the passenger's side rear window causing a squealing alarm to blare.

Howie's eyes widened and his jaw dropped. He cussed.

"Let's go" I said and we ran to Howie's car and waited there.

A minute later Rick dashes outside and discovers his car has been vandalized. He opened the driver's side door and turned the alarm off. He looked soooo angry. He peered up and down the street, no doubt seeking out the culprit. Howie & I ducked down in our seats. It was much too dark to see us in there.

My mother came out and joined Rick a short while later. She hugged herself like she was cold. Good, I thought. Better than all heated up in Rick's apartment! Rick pointed toward the building entrance and appeared to instruct her to return inside. This worried me at first but she trotted out again a few moments later holding Rick's cordless phone. She handed it to him. He dialed a number, pacing by his car like a tiger in a cage.

About 15 minutes later a police car cruised up the street, no siren but the red & blue whirly lights on its roof were lit. Rick waved him over. It pulled up behind Rick's Mustang. The officer spent some time talking to Rick from his car before stepping out to investigate.

"That should spoil their night," I said.

"Glad you're happy," Howie replied. "You're not gonna do this every time she g-goes out with him, are you?"

I glared at him.

"I'm just s-saying, there's g-g-gotta be a better way. Something simpler."

Howie did have a point I hadn't considered. They likely would have other dates in the future and I couldn't keep breaking windows or whatever to foil them. I have to be smarter about this. I told Howie as much.

"You must really hate this guy," he said.

"I don't" I answered honestly. "He's just not right for her."

"Shouldn't your mom b-b-be the one to figure that out?" he asked.

"No" I said, explaining the situation to him as if he were a Lenny. *(Publisher's annot: presumed to be a reference to the "Lennie" character from John Steinbeck's novel OF MICE AND MEN.)* "She's not of sound mind right now. After dallying with so many men, she's become ravenous, an addict. This, Howie, is an intervention."

Howie nodded in understanding then asked "What now?"

I told him he could take me home. He protested, wanting to go get pizza with me or something.

I started rubbing my temples. "I have such a headache," I groaned masterfully. "And cramps. I got my period today. So another time OK?"

Howie consented.

I arrived home 20 minutes later and began penning this entry. Soon afterward I heard Rick's Mustang roar up the block. I peered out my window to watch him drop my mother off. He didn't get out to walk her to our front door. They didn't even kiss each other goodnight!

I listened for my mom trudging up the stairs. I picked up my Jane Eyre book to pretend I had been reading not spying and went to the threshold of my room.

"Hi mom" I said.

"Oh lord what a crazy night," she said.

"Have fun?"

"The dinner was excellent," she replied. "But then someone smashed Rick's car window."

I acted shocked.

"He thinks it was these kids he yelled at yesterday for blasting their music too loud."

"That must've ruined your evening."

"It killed the mood," said mom. "But we'll resurrect that next time."

"Perhaps it was a warning," I said ominously.

"What was?"

"Breaking Rick's window."

"A warning of what?"

"Maybe somebody is out to get Rick," I said. "And then you could be in grave danger too mom."

Mom chuckled. "I don't think so hon."

"What if Rick deals drugs or guns?" I blurted with the direst of demeanors.

My mother scoffed at this. "Rick is not a gangster! If he were, he wouldn't be living in a one bedroom apartment off Hempstead Turnpike."

So she wasn't buying it, but I had to plant the seed of suspicion and fear in her.

"What if next time he's the target of a drive-by shooting? Or somebody blows up his car? You could wind up being killed with him!"

Mom shook her head and theorized all the old movies I watch must be warping my brain. Then she headed into the bathroom across the hall to get ready for bed.

I followed her and stood outside the door.

"Who knows what dark secrets he keeps?" I posed. "He could be like Uncle Charlie in Shadow of a Doubt!"

"What kind of dark secrets could a garbageman have?" mom said through the door.

With dramatic flair I exclaimed "You may not find out until it's too late, Mother! Too late!!!"

I heard my mom turn on the shower. I returned to my room, mildly satisfied.

Indeed tonight's operation had been bold.

But I need to be brilliant.

April 24

Today I launched Phase 2 of my plan, which required a more direct approach.

After school I went home and put on my sexy black dress with mother of pearl buttons and a frilled white collar, much like Joan Crawford wore in Grand Hotel. I stuck a yellow daisy from our garden in my updo. I then rode my bicycle all the way to Rick's. It took almost half an hour to get there but I wasn't tired at all. I was energized by Love!

I leaned my bike against the building and went to the entrance. I found Rick's full name — Rick Fahling — on the directory and rang his apartment.

Over the intercom came Rick's deep voice: "Yeah?"

I cleared my throat and recited the lines I'd rehearsed for him. "Hi Rick. It's Verona Cassidy, Debi's daughter. I need to talk to you."

"OK" he answered. "Wanna come up?"

I said yes and he buzzed me in.

When Rick opened his apartment door my breath caught in my throat. He was wearing jeans and nothing else! His bare chest, ripply muscled, was only a little hairy, just enough to make me want to run my fingers through it. His nipples were dark and hard like candy drops. His tummy was flat, with an inny belly button I wanted to poke. I wondered if he was ticklish.

His hair was damp so I figured he must have just gotten out of the shower. I tried very hard not to imagine myself showering with him. If I had fantasized about that I wouldn't have been able to speak!

"Hi Verona" he said. "How ya doin?"

"Good" I answered, trying to stare into his alluring blue eyes and not at his awesome godlike body, which really wasn't much better for my concentration. I felt awkward. And hot.

"Did I come at a bad time?" I asked him. (Of course I didn't think so!)

"Nope. I just stepped out of the shower. Wanna come in?"

I nodded and entered his sanctuary. It smelled of manly musk and cigarette smoke.

"You sure I'm not imposing?" I said, hoping he would be impressed by how polite and respectful I am.

"Not at all. It's cool. I'm just gonna put on a shirt. Gimme a sec."

Rick went to the kitchen counter and took a drag off a cigarette and mashed it out in the ashtray. He then walked into his bedroom, leaving me alone there.

The walls were beige and the floor was a caramel-colored hardwood and the sofa was white with some yellowish stains on it. There was a lot of baseball collectible stuff. He had a TV and a stereo and a large painting of a nude black lady.

I took his crushed cigarette from the ashtray — it touched his lips! — and put it in my purse.

When Rick returned from the bedroom I was looking at the nude painting on the wall, wondering if his taste leaned toward African women. My mom was as pale pink as me so you can imagine I was quite confused.

Rick slinked up beside me, buttoning up a gray flannel shirt. I wanted so badly to latch my hands onto his beefy bicep, climb up him and wrap my legs around his waist and kiss him until my lips went numb!

"That's the picture from The Shining," he told me. The one in some man's brother's bedroom.

I had no idea what he was talking about but I nodded anyway. My expression though must have given away my ruse.

"Ever see The Shining?" he asked.

"No" I answered.

"Phenomenal movie. You should watch it. I have it on tape. I'll lend it to you sometime if you wanna see it."

Sure I said, still not knowing anything about The Shining other than it was a movie. But I figured if he liked movies then we had something in common.

"Ever see Roman Holiday?" I asked him.

Rick shook his head. "I don't think so."

I told him <u>Roman Holiday</u> is a classic, that it stars Gregory Peck & Audrey Hepburn, and that it's really really romantic.

I gazed up at him, into his eyes, and smiled. He looked down at me. I could see my reflection in his pupils. Neither of us said anything, just stared at each other, a million silent affections passing between us. His adam's apple bobbed as he swallowed. He was so nervous! I knew he wanted me then, but he wouldn't have me. Not yet.

"So you said you needed to tell me something?"

Yes indeed, I thought, let's get down to business, why I'm here. "It's about my mother" I said grimly.

Rick asked me if I wanted to sit down. I sat on the sofa, hoping he would sit next to me but instead he sat on an armchair across from me.

"I was wondering how much my mother told you about herself," I said.

"A bunch of stuff," he replied. "Why?"

I said "You seem like a really sweet guy, Rick. And I don't feel it's fair of her to keep you in the dark."

"About what?" he asked.

I told him that ever since my mother left my father, she's dated lots of men.

Rick says that's normal.

"I mean" I explained "she's slept with lots of men. Dozens." While I was still working from the script in my head, I was telling the truth. Despite my mother's busy schedule she went on 2 or 3 dates a week average, sometimes not coming home from them until the following morning. It was scandalous behavior.

Rick didn't appear at all fazed by this so I embellished.

"She has herpes. And she's HIV positive."

This information hit Rick hard. His jaw tensed and he winced slightly. I felt a little guilty about hurting him. But I didn't feel bad about saying it because while I didn't know for certain if mom had herpes or HIV, she could have them. So it wasn't an outright fib.

"Really?" Rick asked.

"I knew it" I said, feigning disgust. "She didn't tell you."

Rick shook his head.

"My mom has mental problems too," I said truthfully. "She once tried to cut off this guy's you-know-what." That last part I made up to scare him.

Stunned by this revelation, Rick slumped back in his chair, raked his fingers through his beautiful hair, and sighed.

"I don't know what to say. I really dig your mom."

"You know, me & my mom are a lot alike," I said. "Except for the crazy slutty part. You & I could get to know one another better. You can show me that movie with the painting in it. Right now if you want."

Rick looked at me like I was a cat playing too close to the fish bowl.

"You were the one who wrote me those letters, weren't you?"

"Yes, that was me" I confessed — healthy relationships are built on honesty. "But I didn't know you were dating my mother then."

"I think I know what's going on here," he said.

"You do?"

"You're jealous I'm dating your mom."

I pshawed. "Jealous? No. She's just not right for you. You deserve better." He does!

"And that would be you?" he asked. I am!

I rose from the sofa and pressed my palm to my heart. "From the moment I saw you," I declared passionately, "I knew we were meant for each other. There's not a doubt in my mind." I stepped toward him and took a deep breath.

"I love you Rick."

He sighed. "No you don't."

Oh yes I do, I assured him.

"For one thing you don't even know me. And for another, you're like what, 14?"

"15. Almost 16."

"I'm 35" he said. "More than twice your age."

"So?" I said. "That's not a big deal. In some countries, girls as young as 12 marry men as old as 50."

"Listen to me Verona." I love how he says my name, a little raspy with thinly veiled hints of desire. "Nothing's ever gonna happen between us."

"Give me a chance Rick" I pleaded.

He said no.

Please I said.

"I'm just not interested." Then he suggested I leave.

I started to explain myself further so he'd understand it was OK to love me.

"I do understand. And if you go now, I won't tell your mom about this. Though you should be ashamed, making up all that nasty stuff about her."

"I was just trying to warn you."

Rick stood up from his chair and loomed over me, so close I could smell the soap on his body, the cigarettes on his breath. We peered deeply into each other's eyes.

"I think you're a liar," he said. "And I don't want you coming by here ever again. Hear me?"

Rick then steered me to his front door and out of his apartment. He had shut the door on me before I could utter another endearment, another proclamation of my heart's resolve. No time to even bid him farewell.

But fret not, dear fans, I am not discouraged!

When I was biking home I passed the wedding shop on Merrick Ave. In the window there were 2 mannequins, a bride & a groom. I noticed she was missing a hand and he part of his nose. Yet such flaws don't prevent people from falling in love with one another, do they? If imperfect people can fall in love so can Rick & me.

Shakespeare once wrote "The course of true love never did run smooth."

I fear you are under a witch's spell, my love. But I shall break her curse and then each our rivers may flow into one.

April 25

Last night I had a delicious idea. From the hall closet I pulled down 3 shoeboxes full of family photos. There were hundreds, mostly from vacations and holidays. A bunch had been taken before I was born, back to when mom & dad had just gotten married.

I found an empty photo album I could use. I spread the photos on my bed and picked out the happiest pictures of mom & dad together, having fun, where they looked the most in love. Several of their wedding pictures and lots of parties and trips all over the world. I was up working on it most of the night.

Tomorrow when I go to my father's I will present him proof of my mother's enduring love and they will open their hearts to one another once again.

And then Rick will be freed to be with me!

April 26

Mom dropped me off at dad's this morning. It was drizzling and gloomy out but I was super excited to set my plan into motion.

Dad & I had Chinese takeout for lunch. He ordered the moo shu pork, I had the sesame chicken. We ate at the dining room table off bone china plates.

"Do you miss mom?" I asked him.

"Sometimes" he answered. Then, upon pondering the question further, said "Yeah I do."

This was good.

"I think she misses you too."

"Doubt that. After what I put her through I'm surprised she didn't put a hit out on me."

As far as I can remember, my mom & dad ALWAYS argued. They mostly fought about money. (This was before my dad's law firm took off and my mom got her real estate license.) They also fought about the food in the fridge, the dust on the TV, and the hair in the sink. And of course they fought about me. My mom resented having to stay home all day to care for me while my dad went out all the time on alleged business. I was 8 when she found out he was cheating on her with a Russian dancer. Six months later they got divorced.

My mom dove back into the singles scene with a vengeance while my dad kept dating his garden variety bimbos with the fake nails and pumped up hooters.

Neither has had a meaningful relation- ship since they split up. I believe that's because deep down they still desire to rekindle that flame they must have once felt for one another. All they need is the spark to light it again.

I removed the **photo album**[*] from my knapsack and gave it to dad.

[*]ITEM CATALOGED 05/05/1986
NASSAU COUNTY P.D. CASE # 003199
EVIDENCE LOG # 003199-08-3

"What's this?" he asked.

"I found it in mom's room. I caught her staring at it a few days ago. She hides it in her drawer."

"Sounds like she doesn't want you looking at it."

I told him I think he should see it.

"If that's like your mother's diary I know I shouldn't be looking at it."

"Just open it dad. Please."

He stared at the cover. I had glued dried flower petals onto it and spritzed it with my mom's perfume which I hoped she wore when they were together.

"It smells like her" he said.

Good.

Dad opened the book to the first page. It was their wedding photo on the beach. He studied it a while then slowly flipped through the pages. I added some different sized hearts I'd cut from construction paper. Dad didn't say a word until he reached the last picture of them lying beside each other on a hospital bed after I was born, dad's arms wrapped around mom's shoulders, mom holding me swaddled in a white blanket.

"Deb... your mom made this?" he asked. He seemed touched by it, as I hoped he would be.

"Who else would?" I replied.

"Wow. I didn't think she still" Dad didn't finish his sentence.

"She obviously does" I assured him. "You should call her. Maybe you two can get together. See how things go."

I could practically see the gears in my father's brain spinning. Now I just have to wait for him to make his move.

April 27

Still at dad's. Last night I spied him looking at mom's album again. He was sitting in his favorite leather recliner drinking a glass of scotch. He was smiling. It was a good sign.

It then occurred to me I needed to soften up my mother to the idea of dad coming back into her life. So I composed a **love letter**[*] to her from him on his personal computer. I printed out an extra copy to share here

---

[*]ITEM CATALOGED 05/05/1986
NASSAU COUNTY P.D. CASE # 003199
EVIDENCE LOG # 003199-05-1b

Transcription of original accompanying document:

Even when I sleep my thoughts rush to you, my beloved Debi, now and then joyfully, then again sadly, waiting to know whether Fate will hear my prayer. To face life I must live altogether with you

or, impossibly, never remember you. I am resigned to be a wanderer abroad until I can fly into your arms and say that I have again found my true home with you.

I pray for your forgiveness, and for you to believe that I will forever more be faithful to you. No other woman can ever possess my heart. Your love had made me the happiest of men. I need stability and regularity in my life. I need you Debi. Only you. Please open your heart to me once more, and you will never again mistrust my most faithful heart.

Ever yours.
Ever mine.
Ever ours.

Kirk

Publisher's annot: document wording appears to have been appropriated from a correspondence written by Ludwig van Beethoven to his "Immortal Beloved" in 1812.

Mom picked me up from dad's at 4:30. We headed straight home. I gave her the letter over dinner. I think she read it at least twice before she said anything.

"Your father wrote this?" she asked, her eyes welling up.

"Like two weeks ago," I answered. "I found it on his computer. I bet he's too nervous to show it to you. But I thought you should see it."

"To be honest V, I don't even know what to think about this."

"I know dad misses you. He told me so. He's been awfully glum without you."

My mother sighed and asked me if I really thought he's changed?

"I think you should give him a chance mom," I said with all the sincerity I could muster. "For me."

She refolded the letter and thanked me, rose from her chair, went into her bedroom and shut the door. I can hear her crying in there.

Good.

[[BREAK]]

Success!

While I helped my mother clear the dishes, the phone rang. Mom answered it. It was dad.

He asked her out to dinner Friday night. She accepted.

Mom said he sounded sweet. She promptly went upstairs to figure out what dress to wear for the occasion. I suggested the green chiffon one she had worn for her Christmas office party. It's backless with a plunging neckline and a high slit up the leg. It's just the right blend of trashy and tasteful. What dad likes.

I feel like I could dance on a cloud right now!!!

April 28

Mom told him this morning.

While I was getting ready for school I spotted Rick's truck pull up outside to collect our garbage. My mom walked out to meet him in her work clothes. They spoke for less than 5 minutes. Rick looked annoyed but resigned. Poor guy. If he only knew this was best for him!

When mom came back inside I went down-stairs.

"Were you talking to Rick?" I asked.

Yeah, mom said. She told him they had to cool things off between them because of dad.

"How'd he take it?" I asked.

"He understood. He knows your father & I have a history."

"I'm proud of you mom," I said brightly. "And I know everything's going to work out. Like Tracy & Hepburn."

My mother's expression remained skeptical. "Let's not get our hopes up too much V. Our history wasn't all a fairy tale."

"But it can still have a fairy tale ending," I replied.

Mom smiled at that. She has hope. So do I.

April 29

I had the most wonderful dream last night. I was walking to school. The sky suddenly became dark and ominous and there was loud scary thunder. It started to rain heavily. I was getting drenched so I ran up a grassy hill to find shelter. I discovered the ruins of a stone building. I stood beneath its buckling roof, shivering and frightened.

Then Rick appeared at the threshold. He was wearing a white poet's shirt, tight leather breeches, and horse riding boots. I could see his muscular chest through the soaked shirt clinging to his skin. He took me into his strong arms and kissed me passionately, just like in that scene with John Wayne & Maureen O'Hara from The Quiet Man. We made love on the straw floor.

I woke up feeling warm and wet.

[[BREAK]]

Today in art class I began painting a portrait of Rick. It's him from the waist up, wearing an elegant white Renaissance era shirt with ruffled cuffs and a lacy jabot draping from the collar. Although oils have richer colors, I'm using acrylics because they dry much faster and I'm going to give the painting to Rick soon. It will be a surprise.

After Social Studies Howie Gutermuth chased after me in the hall on my way to Bio.

"There's a Vincent Price f-f-film festival at the Gables," he told me. "You wanna go with me?"

I of course didn't. Being seen with Howie in public, even accidentally, would be nothing less than humiliating! And besides, I don't even like Vincent Price very much.

"Can't" I said. "I'm busy."

"They got shows Saturday & Sunday."

"I'm busy all weekend."

"Then how about n-n-next weekend? They got another"

"Listen Howie" I mercifully cut him off. "You're nice and all. But I'm just not interested in you."

"But I like you Verona," Howie whined. "A lot. And you used to like m-m-me, remember?"

Ugh! I remembered. I let him touch my boob in 5th grade. I wanted to forget it ever happened. He didn't, not that I blame him.

"It's time to move on, don't you think?" I proposed. "Besides," I added, "I'm already spoken for."

This put the brakes on his locomotive. "Y-y-you have a b-b-boyfriend?"

I presented him with the most sympathetic look I could. "My heart belongs to another, yes."

Howie nodded, wished us well, and shuffled off.

It's true. The truth shall set me free.

May 1

Finished Rick's painting. I spent the last couple of days working on it for hours after school. I can't wait to give it to him tomorrow! I know he'll love it. Maybe he'll hang it on his wall in place of the nude black lady from the movie. Or above his bed.

The hardest part about painting it was deciding on the background. Originally I was going to make it various shades of green like forest leaves. Then I was thinking about solid black so Rick would best stand out. But I ultimately chose a deep red, the color of hearts, roses, and Love.

My art teacher Mr. Yoches said it looked like Rick was standing in front of a blood waterfall. I'm pretty sure Mr. Yoches is gay. He has no appreciation of romance.

May 2

How many things could go wrong, how many plans derailed, how many hopes dashed?

Tonight, ALL OF THEM!!!

My mom left at 7 on her date with dad. She wore the green dress I recommended. She looked lovely, sexy and sophisticated, like Ava Gardner. I knew dad would like her. I watched when he picked her up from our house in his new silver BMW. He even got out and opened the door for her like a gentleman and gave her a kiss on the cheek. I knew mom would like that.

So far so good.

After they drove off I put on the dress from my junior high prom. It has this rouched bodice and a red over black layered skirt with a big black bow on the hip. It looks fabulous on me and the skirt was short enough so I could ride my bicycle in it without a problem. (The last dress I wore had gotten caught in the spokes.)

I fetched Rick's painting from my closet. I strapped it to my bike's rack and pedaled over to his place. I carried the painting up to the entrance and buzzed his apartment.

"Yeah?" Rick said from the speaker. His voice was a little staticky.

"Hi Rick" I sang into the intercom. "It's Verona."

"What's up?" he asked.

I asked him if I could see him.

"I told you I didn't want you dropping by here anymore."

"I know" I replied. "But it's important." I told him I had a surprise for him.

There was a long pause before he answered.

"Gimme a few minutes. I'll come down to you."

I said OK and waited.

20 minutes later Rick finally struts out in a baby blue blazer and crisp black pants. He looked great! He looked ready to hit the hot spots in town. I hoped he would ask me to join him.

"What do you want?" he asked me.

"I want to give you this." I showed him the painting.

His face expressed nothing. He just said it wasn't bad. But he didn't say it was good.

My smile dissolved into a frown. "You don't like it?"

He told me he didn't want it.

"But I painted it for you."

He said he didn't ask me to.

"Of course you didn't," I said. "That's what makes it a surprise, silly."

"Go home Verona."

He may as well have slapped me across the cheek. Did he hate the painting that much?

"Why?" I asked him. "What's wrong?"

"You're what's wrong" he said. "Go find someone your own age to date. Someone you can relate to. Whoever. Just quit g-d damn bothering me. Is that clear enough?"

I stood there speechless, in a daze.

Rick hated ME

He marched to his car and got in. He started the engine and sped away, tires screeching on the pavement. It hurt my ears.

I pressed the painting to my bosom for a while. Then I smashed it against the stairs, over & over & over, until it was utterly and thoroughly destroyed.

Like my heart, dear fans.

I went home and sobbed for a long time in my room. Even when the rain of tears stopped, the gray clouds remain over me.

Then my mother came back. My dad wasn't with her.

She went upstairs. I stepped out of my room to see her. I was pretty curious about her date with dad and I welcomed the diversion from Rick.

Mom didn't look happy.

"How'd it go?" I asked her.

"It was OK" she said.

"Are you going out again?"

She sighed. "I don't think so V. Your father & I have obviously grown apart. Tonight just showed us how much."

I told her that stinks.

"I know sweetie. I'm sorry."

I wasn't really surprised. And it doesn't matter now anyway.

"Why are your eyes so red?" mom asks me. "Have you been crying?"

"A little" I answer. A little if you compared my tears with the Atlantic Ocean!

My mother then hugged me. She doesn't really ever do that. It felt weird but kind of nice too.

"Oh my poor baby. Anything you want to talk about?"

"No" I said. "It's stupid."

"If something makes you cry, it's not stupid."

I shrugged in her arms.

"Well, anytime you want to chat V, I'm here for you. Alright?"

I nodded and started sniffling again and hugged her back. We held each other for a while, two sad souls that Love has abandoned. I never felt closer to her.

May 3

This morning I spent 2 hours doing my makeup. Or rather, doing it, undoing it, and redoing it again. I couldn't get me to look right. My eyes look tired, my cheeks puffy, my lips thin. I plucked too much off my eyebrows. My hair is a rat's nest no rat would ever live in. My mirror shows me a horror movie in which I am the star. I am the Bride of Frankenstein. But not even Frankenstein's monster could love me like this.

What if I'm not beautiful? What if I've never been beautiful?

Maybe I belong with everybody else. I'm nothing special. I'm just another ugly person living in uglyville.

Who will EVER want me?

Who will EVER want me?

Who will EVER want me?

Who will EVER want me?

Who will EVER want me?

Who will

The text hereunder has been transcribed from Verona Cassidy's original personal journal, written during her incarceration in the Nassau County Juvenile Corrections Center, acquired by the Publisher on February 27, 2014.

So much to tell, dear fans! The last few weeks have been a roller coaster ride of drama & action & suspense & intrigue & yes, Romance!

Where to resume my story?... The day Ricky returned to my house. At the time he was still under my mother's curse. I was in my room when I heard his Mustang rumble up outside. He rang the doorbell and my mother let him in. I crept out of my room and listened from the stairs. Mom & Ricky were talking about getting hamburgers at All American then driving down to Lido Beach. It was a beautiful day, too beautiful for them to be enjoying together, my mother conjuring up new bewitching memories to trap him more in her web.

I needed to do something or I would lose my Ricky forever!

I stepped into the living room where they were getting ready to leave.

"Hello" I said. My mom smiled at me. Ricky didn't.

Mom said "Hey V. Up finally?"

"I've been up a couple of hours putting on my face."

Mom asks me if I remember Rick.

"Yes" I answer and say "Hi Rick."

Ricky nodded at me. We locked eyes for a moment and I could tell — even though my mother claimed him as hers — that he still desired ME. Dear fans, the eyes never lie! His pupils enlarged and his steel blue irises twinkled at the sight of me. I then knew I still had a chance. We still had a chance!

"Where are you going?" I innocently asked though I already knew where.

"Just out to lunch," my mother replied. "Then a walk on the boardwalk. Maybe play a game of pitch n putt."

"How delightful" I said, giving my voice a trace of worry. Then as I stared at Ricky I said "Can I speak to you in private, mom?"

My mother nodded and we went into the kitchen together while Ricky waited in the living room. I'm certain he knew I was plotting something and he didn't stop me. Another sign he wanted us to be reunited, wanted me to break my mother's spell over him.

In the kitchen I tell my mother that Ricky & I are in love.

Mom didn't believe me at first, doing that thing with her mouth that looks like she just tasted something sour. "What are you talking about?" she asked.

"We've been seeing each other for a while now. Since before you met him. We haven't told anyone. It's been our secret."

Mom scoffed. "You can't be serious?"

I nodded. "He feels bad that you're all alone and he wanted to help you feel better, show you a fun time now & then.

He's very compassionate like that. But he doesn't love you. Only me."

The truth can be so hurtful. My mother's lips fluttered as it sank in and took root. Then she stormed out of the kitchen.

"Mother, don't!" I called after her. "You'll embarrass him. Just tell him you have to end it." But she was beyond being reasonable about this.

I followed her back into the living room. My mother stood in front of Ricky, crossing her arms like she does when she's about to explode but trying to hold it in.

"My daughter says you two have been seeing one another. Romantically."

Ricky gazed at me with a look that said, How clever you are Verona!

But he said "No Debi. Verona just has a crush on me."

I was kind of surprised Ricky would not profess his love for me since it would've solved everything right then & there. But I figure I had ambushed him with my scheme so he denied it on reflex. He probably didn't want to upset my mom because he's such a goodhearted soul who only wishes to make everybody happy even though that's impossible.

My mother regarded me dubiously. I could tell she wanted to believe Ricky instead of her own daughter because she wanted Ricky for herself. Mom can be selfish like that.

I thought fast and blurted "We made love on his sofa under the picture of the naked black lady."

"You had sex with my daughter, you son of a b---h?!"

"No I didn't! She's lying!"

My mother glared at Ricky like a burbling angry volcano.

"Listen to me" Ricky said, "She dropped by my place once uninvited, but I demanded she leave."

"And you didn't tell me this why?"

"I.. I.." Ricky stammered, "just.. didn't."

Ricky wasn't helping us so I helped him out.

"It's OK Rick" I said. "We don't have to hide our love any longer."

Ricky looked at me then at my mother. "She's insane. This is all in her head." He was really putting on a convincing performance though I wasn't sure why. "Debi, I wouldn't"

"Get the f--k out of my house, Rick." I seldom hear my mother drop the f bomb but when she does it packs a wallop.

"You can't be swallowing this," Ricky said.

Then my mother did something I would never have expected of her. She grabbed the iron poker by the fireplace and pointed it at Ricky.

"Go now or I swear I'm going to stick this in you and I guarantee it'll feel a lot less pleasant than what you did to my little girl."

I leapt in front of Ricky to shield him and shouted "No mother!"

"I didn't do anything with her!" Ricky insisted. "Please believe me."

"Why should I?" my mother answered him, her voice now ice cold and brimming with menace. "I hardly even know you, do I?"

Ricky tossed his hands up in mock surrender. But I knew he knew we had triumphed over the Wanton Witch! "OK. That's the way it's gonna be. Fine. I'm out of here."

"Rick! Wait!" I tried to grasp his arm but he jerked it away and snarled at me and charged out of the house.

"Verona!!!" my mother screamed at me. She thrust the poker into the couch cushion. She was mad in both senses of the word.

"Please don't be angry," I said.

Mom exhaled a calming down breath. "I don't blame you V. You're only 15. He's the disgusting pervy pedophile."

I started to protest her remark, to defend my Ricky's honor, when I saw my mother reach for the phone.

I asked who she was calling?

"The police. You're underage. That's rape."

I panicked. Ricky getting arrested was not part of my plan.

"Don't you dare, mother!"

"He used you, V. He should go to jail."

"No he shouldn't!" Jail?? That was NOT going to happen! "I won't testify against him. Never ever."

Despite my objection mom began to dial.

"We'll just run away together," I said.

That stopped my mother's fingers. But it refueled her fury. "The hell you will!" she snapped at me.

I kept my composure. "Then leave us alone. Let us fan the flames of our love."

"You're going back to therapy."

I told her she was overreacting.

"I'm calling your father. I'm sure he'll have something to say about this."

I was sure he would too, though nothing that would matter. But I didn't want my mother further stirring this boiling pot lest it spill over and burn us horribly. I said dad wouldn't understand.

"Well neither do I!" mom shot back. She ordered me to my room and told me to stay there until she sorted stuff out. Then she picked up the phone again.

I needed to find Ricky before my parents had a chance to talk things through. I wasn't sure what they would do but it was bound not to be good. I didn't foresee them giving Ricky & me their blessing. No doubt they would drive a wedge between us, send him to prison or me to boarding school or both. So I raced out of the house. Mother yelled after me but she didn't chase me beyond the front stoop. I ran like my life depended on it (Which it did!) As I turned the corner at the end of my block, I could see my mother still outside talking on the cordless phone.

Then I ran even harder to my Ricky.

I scarcely remember my full speed, many mile sprint to Ricky's. I bumped into Howie Gutermuth when I passed the ice cream parlor. He wanted to chat but I told him I was in a rush. He offered to give me a ride. I pretended not to hear him and kept going. Sure I would've gotten to Ricky's quicker but then I would've had to figure out a way to ditch Howie without dealing with 101 questions from him.

I made it to Ricky's apartment building within minutes. Though my hair and clothes were a mess those were the least of my concerns. I took a moment to catch my breath. When an old lady walking a little white dog came out the entrance I slipped inside past her.

I knocked on Ricky's door. He answered it and scowled at me.

"Jesus. What the hell do you want from me?"

He must have still been cross I had sprung my plan on him without warning but there were more important matters to address now.

"We have to talk" I said. "Things have gotten out of hand."

"Oh really? I wonder how that happened."

I started crying. "I know what I did was dumb. Dumber than dumb. I don't know what made me say all that stuff and I don't know what to do about it now."

He suggested telling my mother the truth.

I shook my head. "She's too flustered to listen. She wanted to call the cops."

Ricky barked the lord's name in vain.

"But I stopped her from doing it. And then she tried calling my dad."

One of Ricky's neighbors exited her apartment while I was still out on his doorstep sobbing like some wretched orphan. So Ricky invited me inside and shut the door behind me. I still loved how manly it smelled in there, like the men's locker room at my dad's country club.

"I didn't mean for any of this to happen," I said. "Honest."

"What did you expect? You thought you could just make up a relationship between us, and then what? We'd live happily ever after?"

"I didn't want my mother to have you. I wanted you for myself. I saw you first, I deserve you more."

"Man, you're a piece of work." At first I thought Ricky was impressed by my passion and commitment but then I realized he really was upset at me for doing what I did. Maybe he had been close to his own mother and thought what I did to my mom was mutinous and disrespectful. He is obviously a man with strong family values. He'll be a great father to our children.

I said "Oh you must think I'm so horrible."

"Right now I think you need to make this right," he said. "You have to tell your folks I never screwed around with you."

Ricky was right. I had not conceived this plan carefully enough. There was too much at stake if things got worse. So I promised him I would tell my parents the truth as soon as they calmed down. But he didn't want to wait. He wanted it straightened out right then & there.

"Trust me, they won't listen when they're this mad," I said.

"I don't give a crap how mad they are. I'm beyond p.o.ed!"

I told him not to worry. I swore I would make things right.

Then his front door buzzer buzzed. Ricky went over to the speaker box on the wall and pressed the talk button.

"Is this Rick?" I recognized the voice immediately. "This is Verona's father. Let me in."

Ricky was very not happy but he let my dad up. He then turned to me and said "Verona, if you care about me as much as you say you do, you'll tell your dad the truth OK?"

Just as I nodded there was a knock on Ricky's door. He opened it and my father stepped inside and looked at me critically. I guess I must've looked like a wreck. I can't imagine what he must have been thinking but it wasn't anything good.

"Go home V" my father said. "Rick & I have matters to discuss."

"She should stay" Ricky said. "You need to hear"

Dad told him he needed to shut up. I could tell he was drunk. Not stumbling drunk but mean drunk. He told me to go home again.

"I can't" I replied.

"Can't or won't?"

Ricky interjected "Let's just chill out here. It's Kirk, right?"

My father nodded slightly, his hands clenched into fists. My whole body tensed up. Dad was a powder keg poised to explode. I didn't want to be around for that but I wasn't abandoning Ricky to bear the brunt of my father's unbridled wrath.

"There's been a mistake," Ricky said.

"Yeah, you made one colossal mother f--king mistake."

Ricky said he didn't do anything.

"What kind of creep are you?" my father asked him. (I doubt he was really expecting an answer.) "You date single mothers so you can seduce their teenage daughters?"

"No I don't" Ricky insisted. "Tell him Verona."

Dear fans, I was faced with quite the quandary. If I told the truth I could lose Ricky forever. But if I told the untruth I would not be able to live with myself.

"Go on" Ricky urged me.

I chose to go with the Truth and let Destiny decide the consequences.

"Dad" I said and took a deep breath before declaring "I love him! And Ricky loves me!"

Ricky called me an evil b---h. It had hurt me then but I don't condemn him now for calling me that. At that moment he was under a lot of stress and very confused about his feelings.

My father however was far less con-fused about what he felt about Ricky calling me that nasty name. He punched Ricky in the mouth! Ricky staggered back-wards a couple of steps and wiped a trickle of blood dripping from his bottom lip. He looked angry.

He said "Get out of my apartment, both of you."

Father stubbornly said that he was going to do no such thing.

Ricky repeated his request, adding or else he would throw dad out.

Dad didn't budge. Whenever he had his brain set on something, he always dug in his heels. But this was Ricky's castle and he wasn't going to let my father seize it.

Ricky snagged him by the shirt collar and tried pushing him toward the door. Dad swiped Ricky's arm away and threw another punch to his jaw but missed. Then they grappled like sumo wrestlers and tumbled over the sofa.

I screamed NO!!! at my father.

While he pinned Ricky to the floor dad grabbed the glass ashtray from the coffee table and tried to smash Ricky in the head with it. Ricky knocked him off and they both sprang to their feet. Dad hurled the ashtray at Ricky. It just missed him, shattering against the wall. Dad then snatched up a baseball bat that was leaning in the corner. He took a wide swing at Ricky who dodged it by bending backward.

I leapt in front of Ricky and shouted "Stop it!" But dad was already swinging the bat again and hit me in the shoulder. I squealed in dreadful pain and spun away from Ricky.

"Rosebud?" I heard my father say, sounding appalled by what he had done.

Ricky lunged and tackled my father. They toppled over the sofa again and landed hard on the hardwood floor. Something made a CRAAACK noise. Ricky rolled off my father. Dad wasn't moving. His head was twisted at an unnatural angle.

"Daddy?" I said. I hadn't called him daddy in years.

Ricky looked stunned. "I think he broke his neck."

I asked Ricky if my father was dead though I knew he must be. His eyes were still wide open and looking directly at me but not at <u>me</u>. He was peering into that next world beyond the veil. I knelt down beside him and stroked his hair, something I remembered he did to me when I was little and suffered bad headaches. But then I just couldn't look at him anymore so I put a magazine over his face.

At first I couldn't help thinking this was all my fault. Then I realized my father shared fault too. He always was over-protective and short-tempered. He came there to beat up Ricky, maybe even kill him. Ricky had only been defending himself!

Ricky was really upset and pacing the room. He kept apologizing to me, saying he didn't mean to do it. I told him I knew he didn't mean it. He collapsed into his chair and buried his face in his palms. He agonized about his neighbors reporting the ruckus to the police though nobody ever came.

"They're going to throw me in jail again for this! And I ain't going to get out this time. This is a life sentence."

"It was an accident" I said.

"It was a fight" he replied.

"It was self-defense. He attacked you. I'm a witness."

"Yeah, your word should go over real f--king well."

Ricky was in an extremely emotional state. He appeared to be on the verge of tears. I felt so bad for him. I crawled over to him, placed my hands on his knees and rubbed them. My shoulder still stung from the bat but I paid it no mind.

"We can make this right Ricky," I assured him. "We just have to work together."

He said that he didn't want to do anything with me.

I said "What choice do you have?"

Then he gazed into my eyes and knew I was right.

Now I don't want you all to think I am cold hearted and didn't care about the tragedy just befallen my father. I loved him as much as I could. After my parents divorced he wasn't around for me a lot and when I did see him he often treated me like an unwelcome distraction from whatever else he needed or wanted to do. He occasionally tried though. He generally acted interested in my life (never enough to actually understand it) and seemed to enjoy eating out with me at really nice restaurants. He gave me nice gifts for my birthdays and Christmas. He even once brought me a fresh skirt at school after I'd soiled mine during lunch period. So I realize I should have been mourning the flawed but sometimes thoughtful Kirk Cassidy. But there was <u>nothing</u> I could do about his demise.

Ricky however needed my help and I wasn't going to let him down!

Ricky wrapped my father in a bedsheet while I cleaned up and wiped down anything in the apartment he may have touched. My mother called Ricky while we were doing this. He didn't pick up his phone so she left a message on his answering machine.

"This is Debi" she said. "Verona's missing. She hasn't been home since you left here. If you know where she is, if she's there, please tell her to come home. Or call me. I just want to know she's OK. Please Rick. Do the right thing."

After Ricky tied off the ends of the bedsheet with a pair of athletic socks, he lit a cigarette and called my mother back. He told her no, I wasn't there but he would call her if he saw me. After he hung up he sank down into his chair. He was quiet for a while then asked me "How can you be so cheerful?"

I wasn't. I was totally nervous. When I get nervous I whistle to myself, in this instance the song "Only You" by the band Yaz. Which sounds like a happy song, even though it's about heartbreak I think.

"Your father is lying there dead on the floor rolled up in a sheet," Ricky said.

"I know" I replied.

"That's your f--king dad!"

I guess Ricky was puzzled by how well I was handling the situation. He probably expected me to be fraught with anguish, on my knees and bawling my eyes out like Maria at the end of West Side Story. But I hadn't cried at all.

"He was my dad once," I explained. "He hasn't been a dad to me for a long time."

Ricky just shook his head.

I then said "What's important now is keeping you out of trouble."

Ricky huffed and chuckled at the same time. "Yeah, well, trouble always finds a way of biting me on the ass."

"You said you were in jail before. Why?"

"I ran this guy over with my truck. Crippled him." He paused to suck on his cigarette. "Spent 7 years in the slammer for it."

My poor beloved! I can't fathom what it must have been like for him locked away all those years in a concrete box. "That must've been terrible for you."

"I ain't keen on going back."

"You won't" I promised him. "I won't let you."

Late that night I crept out of Ricky's building, checking to see if the coast was clear. It was. I signaled Ricky that it was OK to come out so he did with my shrouded father slung over his shoulder. It looked like Ricky was carrying a giant tootsie roll. I unlocked the trunk of dad's BMW parked out front. Ricky, wearing leather gloves and a Mets baseball cap, quickly laid my father inside and shut it. Then we got in and drove away.

I came up with the idea of disposing of everything in Lake Ronkonkoma. It's a huge kettle lake formed by glaciers hundreds of thousands of years ago. I learned about it in Science class. Some say it's bottomless and that there's a whirlpool in the middle that drags people down into it where they're never seen again.

"You sure this lake's deep enough?" Ricky asked me on the way.

"Yes" I reassured him. "Bet it hides lots of secrets."

"As long as our secret stays hidden down there."

I knew it would. And Ricky would owe his freedom to me.

I was navigating using a road map Ricky had of Long Island and NYC. It took about half an hour to reach the lake. We drove around to the south side where there were no houses or street lights, just trees. We found a steep sandy bank that led straight to the water. We parked at the far end of it. Ricky shifted the car into neutral and told me to get out. Then he got out too and got behind the car. He pushed it until the car was rolling on its own. It dropped off the edge of the bank and plunged into the lake with a splash. Problem solved.

Or so we thought.

We stood there beside one another watching the car slowly sink in the misty moonglow. I felt like we should be holding hands. We were now eternally bound by criminal circumstance, like Lana Turner & John Garfield in The Postman Always Rings Twice. I wound my arm around Ricky's. He didn't shoo me away! I could've stayed there forever but I knew we shouldn't.

"What do you want to do now?" I asked him.

"I wanna go home" he replied. "Forget any of this ever happened."

I said I was famished and suggested we get a bite to eat on the way home.

Ricky thought it best we not be seen together.

I was fine with that. I could just stay at his place and never ever leave.

But Ricky said no. He didn't want to even risk someone spotting me going into his apartment.

"For how long?" I asked.

"Until I'm sure this has all blown over. Which could be a while."

I was crushed. After all we had been through together and I couldn't be with him until who knows when. I felt Fate was teasing me. I felt cheated. I earned him!!!

I tried reassuring him. "I really don't think there's anything to worry about."

That was when Ricky said "I think it stopped sinking."

I peered out at the lake. Just the rear fender of the BMW was still poking out of the water surrounded by dying bubbles.

"It's almost under," I said.

We watched a little while longer. Soon the bubbles had completely stopped and I realized Ricky was right. The car's butt hadn't gone any deeper. It reminded me of a gravestone, which it kind of was.

Ricky shook his head. "S--t! It did stop! It ain't bobbing no more at all. It couldn't of hit bottom, could it?"

"Shouldn't have" I said. "It's a kettle lake."

"Yeah you told me." I liked that Ricky listened to me. "It must've gotten stuck on something," he said.

Then Ricky stripped off his shoes and socks and shirt and leapt into the dark water. He swam the few feet to the car. First he tried to shake and shove the car with his arms but it wouldn't budge. Then floating on his back he kicked at it hard with his powerful legs. It still didn't move. He dove underwater and finally came up two or three minutes later. I was relieved he hadn't drowned.

"What are you doing?" I called to him.

He swam back to shore. I offered him my hand to help him out of the water but he didn't need it. He flopped onto the ground and sat there slouched in the dirt.

"What were you doing?" I asked again.

"I was trying to open the trunk to get your dad out and find someplace else to put him. But then I realized it wouldn't matter. I'm f--ked."

Ricky kept his head bowed all the while he spoke. He looked defeated. I sat down beside him and caressed his arm. His skin was cold and goosebumped from the lake but my hands were warm. I hoped they made him feel better. I hoped he believed I was there for him and always would be.

We walked several minutes down a dark desolate road. I tried to make conversation but Ricky was brooding. I tried talking about school, about my classes, about how Ellen Goldfarb was only popular because she let Calhoun's entire football team have their lecherous way with her. Ricky didn't respond to anything I said but I understood. He had quite a lot on his mind and he wasn't happy his cigarettes got soaked from his dip in the lake.

And then I said "We should run away together. Disappear somewhere."

"Where do you expect to disappear to?" he asked me.

"Anywhere we want" I answered. London, Paris, Rome

"I'm gonna be a wanted man soon. And I'm pretty sure they're gonna be looking high & low for you too. Just a matter of time before they find us."

"Then we just have to go someplace where they can never ever find us." I fantasized about us living on an uncharted desert isle kissing on the beach like Burt Lancaster & Deborah Kerr did in <u>From Here To Eternity</u>.

"You let me know what that place is," Ricky said "and I'll meet you there."

I laughed and told him I would never leave him again!

We stumbled upon a roadside motel called the Sleep Tight Motor Inn. There were only a couple of cars and a pickup truck parked outside. It was quiet and secluded and the neon sign said it was only $29 a night and had HBO.

Ricky fished a $50 bill from his wallet and told me to rent us a room while he got us some food and drinks. He said he was beat and needed time to think.

"One room?" I asked.

"Yeah" he said. "Unless you're uncomfortable with that?"

I said it was fine. Perfect.

He told me to meet him by the snack machines after. I went to the motel office. The lobby was tiny and smelled like stale cigarette smoke. In the corner there was a dusty potted plant wrapped in silver garland. A handwritten note taped to the check-in window informed guests their cable TV wasn't working. Ordinarily this would have disappointed me but I didn't care. I wasn't planning on watching TV with Ricky!

The clerk, this skeletally geezer with an atrocious hairpiece, asked me if I was with anybody (I said my boyfriend) and how long I was staying for (I said one night, what was left of it). He then instructed me to sign the check-in book. I asked him if he really needed my name. He said it could be mine, my boyfriend's, my grand-ma's — it didn't matter to him as long as there was a signature. So I signed it "Jane Rochester" which I thought was pretty clever.

After I paid the clerk gave me the room key and told me to "play it safe" and that the vending machines sold rubbers, which I thought was rather presumptuous of him. But maybe that was normal customer service there.

Ricky bought us a bunch of snacks and sodas. I helped him carry them to our room, which was on the other side of the building. This pleased Ricky. I told him check-out time was at noon. He said we would be gone long before then.

We entered our room. Fake wood paneling covered the walls. The TV was bolted to the top of the bureau. There was a round table with two chairs and a queen sized bed.

Ricky immediately drew the curtains over the window. I turned on a lamp.

"There's only one bed" I said.

"You can have it" he said. "I'll sleep on the floor."

"But look, it's big enough for three people." I hopped onto the bed to show him. "Plenty of room!"

"Plenty of room on the floor too."

I knew Ricky was just being a gentleman. It wasn't proper to sleep with a lady on the first date, even if all we were doing was sleeping. But oh how I was wishing he would let his inner cad out for me. I wouldn't have objected in the slightest.

Ricky took a seat at the table and started eating a bag of Fritos. I sat down on the other chair across from him. He told me I should eat something because we hadn't eaten for hours so I opened a bag of Cheez Doodles. Ricky asked me if I wanted a Coke. I nodded and he popped the tabs on two cans and slid one towards me. I thanked him, smiling. He was being sooo sweet.

Ricky said the motel reminded him of ones his father & him used to stay at when they were on the road together.

"On the road where?" I asked.

"He sold electric shavers out of a suitcase," he told me. "They were pieces of junk but he could talk them up like they were the cuttingest edge technology instead of a fire hazard."

"What was your father like?"

Ricky mulled the question over for a moment before answering. "When I was 7, he once locked me in the trunk of his Cadillac 'cause he caught me stealing a dollar from his wallet. It was pitch black in there and he told me the rats were gonna bite chunks out of me. I was scared s--tless. He kept me in there for 6 hours. That was what my father was like."

"That sounds horrible. Didn't your mom care when he did that?"

"She died in a fire when I was a baby. At least that's what my old man said. But who knows?"

I was glad Ricky was opening up to me and I felt I should reciprocate. I told him about my parents divorce, about how my mother ousted my father from our house when she discovered he was having an affair.

"Must have been rough for you," Ricky said.

"It was hardly a shock" I said. "They always fought, often in front of me or when I was upstairs in my room. I hated hearing them bicker so I'd watch the classic movie channel on TV to drown them out."

"Why old movies?" Ricky asked.

"I used to watch them with my Grammy all the time," I answered. "We both loved the dialogue and the costumes. Grammy used to be in show business. She was a star once." I almost started crying then. Grammy lived with mom & me the summer before her cancer took her. But I don't want to remember her as sick, only as a Star.

"And I like the happy endings," I added.

"Don't we all," Ricky said then peeked out the curtains.

Once Ricky satisfied himself no SWAT team was gearing up to bust down our door, we got ready for bed. He lent me his button shirt to sleep in instead of my dirty skirt. It was long enough on me to reach the middle of my thighs and it had his manly scent which made me want to be closer to him even more.

When I came out of the bathroom I saw Ricky had undressed down to nothing but his baby blue boxer shorts! Dear fans, I thought I was in heaven! Everything I had dreamed about was coming true!!!

He took the floral comforter off the bed and spread it out onto the floor. I sat down on the bed with my knees bent so he could get a glimpse of my black bikini panties if he was so inclined to look. He got an extra blanket from the closet and one of the pillows off the bed. Then he laid down on the comforter and made himself comfortable.

I said I felt bad.

"About what?" Ricky asked. "Taking the bed?"

"About everything" I said. "Well almost everything." I gave him my best come hither stare.

He didn't respond to it. He said "Let's try to get some sleep, OK? It's been a heck of a day for both of us." Then he turned off the lamp on the nightstand. I slipped under the sheets. I tried to watch Ricky but all I could see was the darkness.

The next morning I showered and put on my same outfit I had on the day before. While I was blowdrying my hair I examined myself in the bathroom mirror. I hadn't brought my beauty bag with me so I was looking quite the plain jane. I pinched my cheeks to flush the red out of them and pinched my lips until they looked fuller, which hurt but it was worth it to look good for Ricky.

When I was all done in the bathroom I found Ricky at the table, fully dressed including his shirt which I gave back to him. He was munching on potato chips and smoking a cigarette which he had bought from the cigarette machine.

"You look nice" he said.

"Without my makeup or a brush, a girl does what she can," I said.

"You're lucky. You're naturally pretty."

I'm sure I must have blushed at that! I smiled and thanked him for the compliment.

A siren wailed outside, passing the motel. Ricky peeped through the curtains. Another siren whizzed by.

"Damn" Ricky said. "They probably found the car."

"Maybe not. It could be anything."

Ricky stood and paced the room. "Yeah, guess they could be responding to something else." He was able to calm himself down. "Tell you what," he then said to me, "why don't you go and get us some more snacks?"

"Sure darling" I answered. I didn't really mean to call him that — it just slipped out — but it felt right and Ricky didn't seem to mind at all.

He gave me five dollars. "I'm gonna call my buddy on the pay phone, have him check out my apartment for cops. In case your mom did call them."

"She wouldn't have" I said.

"Well I would've if my daughter didn't come home last night."

I got us food and drinks while Ricky spoke to his friend. When we both got back to the room we ate our breakfasts. He had a pack of coffee cakes and I had chocolate frosted mini donuts.

After we finished eating Ricky showed me how to play Tabletop Football. One person creates a goal with their hands and the other "kicks" a wad of paper by snapping their fingers on it, trying to aim it between the other's goal posts. If they succeed it's a touchdown and they get a point. Ricky was excellent at the game.

"What's the score?" I asked after we'd been playing for a while.

"17 to 3."

"Ew. That's sucky huh?"

"You ain't ready to go pro yet, I can tell you that."

"I'd probably be easy to tackle too. You could hold me down and do whatever you wanted with me."

Yes, I was being brazen! It must have been the sugar rush from the donuts and apple juice.

Ricky said he doesn't tackle women.

"Pity" I said.

There is only so much drubbing a woman can tolerate so I suggested we watch TV. Ricky said OK. I turned it on but forgot the motel's cable was out of order. I managed to find a UHF station with a pretty clear picture.

Roman Holiday was on!!!

"What's that?" Ricky asked.

"That movie with Gregory Peck & Audrey Hepburn I told you about."

"Sorry" he replied, shaking his head. "I don't remember."

I sat down on the edge of the bed in front of the set. "It's near the beginning," I said. "You should see it."

Ricky got up from the table and regarded the TV screen distastefully. "It's black & white."

"It's a classic. Come sit with me."

I patted the space on the bed next to me. Ricky accepted my invitation without reservation. His hip was touching mine! I had to try my hardest to keep the conversation going, to keep from smothering him with smooches. Had I lost control over my simmering desires he wouldn't have been able to stop me!

I explained the film to him. "Audrey Hepburn is this royal princess visiting Italy but she's grown weary of all her diplomatic duties and decorum. All she wants is to experience the life and adventures of a regular person."

"You mean a poor person?" Ricky asked.

"I mean one who doesn't have to answer to anybody but herself."

"What does she care? She's rich."

I told him to just watch and that's what we did. An hour and a half later the movie ended and Ricky hadn't gotten up at all. He didn't even fidget during it.

"Did you like it?" I asked him.

"Yeah" he said. "Except the guy didn't get the girl at the end."

I told him that was because they're from two different worlds. It would never work out.

"More like her stuck-up family would never allow it."

"The point is," I continued, "she got the chance to live how everybody else lives for a little while. And Gregory Peck got to fall in love with a princess."

"It didn't go anywhere though. They played each other and split when the game was over."

"But it was romantic."

"Sure" Ricky scoffed. "While it lasted."

I admit I was a tad peeved Ricky didn't appreciate the charm and magic of Hepburn & Peck's relationship. Yes they were living a fantasy and it was only temporary, but sometimes it's the fleeting things that make life worth living. 'Tis better to have loved and lost than never to have loved at all, the poem goes. But I believe, even if they couldn't be together, Princess Ann & Joe would love one another for evermore.

I turned off the TV. Ricky must have noticed I was kind of annoyed at him.

"I enjoyed it though" he said. "It was cool."

That made me feel better. "Good" I said. "I'm glad you liked it."

And then, dear fans, something super amazing happened!

Ricky groaned and rubbed his shoulder.

"What's wrong?" I asked him.

"Sleeping on the floor last night must've stiffened me up."

"I can help with that," I said. I then scurried up behind him on my knees on the bed and began massaging his shoulders.

He moaned. "That feels incredible."

"I practice on my mom," I told him. "She stresses out a lot." Which was an understatement. She stresses out about everything.

"With you as a daughter, I can imagine why."

"Ha Ha" I said and gently tugged his hair.

"Ow" he said.

"That's what you get for being a smart aleck."

"I was kidding."

"It wasn't funny."

"It sorta was."

"Do you want this massage or not?"

"Yeah" he answered. "I want it bad."

The way he said that made me quivery.

"Then hush" I said and returned to kneading his back. He moaned some more. His shirt kept bunching up and I kept having to smooth it out. This irritated me.

"Ugh!" I finally blurted. "Take off your shirt."

Ricky did. My heartbeat quickened beating quick as a hummingbird's wings and I held my breath to keep from hyper-ventilating.

I explored every curve and cleft of his shoulders, arms, muscles, ribs, spine. It was like my hands were sculpting his supple flesh. My fingertips tingled as they glided over his milky skin. He electrified me — he was a battery and I was his toy ready to be played with any way he wanted.

"That better?" he said.

Uh huh. Much.

After a few minutes my hands and wrists got crampy but I didn't want to stop so I drew my knuckles down and across Ricky's back.

"You can stop now," he said. "Your hands must be tired."

"It's OK" I said. "I don't mind." Not at all!

Ricky stretched his arms and swiveled his body.

"Feels a lot better. Thanks Verona."

"You're welcome."

He turned around to face me and said "I owe you."

I wondered what he meant by that. But I didn't have to wonder for long.

He told me to give him my feet.

"What?" I said.

"Scoot back and put your dogs in my lap."

I did. He then started rubbing my feet. His hands were strong and it felt positively divine! I shut my eyes and basked in his expert touch.

"You like?" he asked.

I mmm hmmm'd.

I get all hot and bothered just thinking about what happened next so writing about it without this pencil going all wacky-doodly is tough. But I will do my best, dear fans. I know you want to hear every-thing!

Ricky massaged the arch of my left foot (he had finished with my right one) then worked down to the heel, then up to the ball and toes. He treated them with reverence, like he was performing some sacred ritual honoring his goddess. He didn't speak the whole time he was doing it. I figured he was just really focused on the task. Then his hand moved from my foot to my calf, cupping it, caressing it. Then he drifted further up my leg, underneath my skirt, inching up my inner thigh, closer, closer, closer...

Then he jerked his hand away.

So close! I could've screamed!!!

"Oh don't stop" I pleaded.

Ricky rose from the bed and ran his fingers through his hair. He looked embarrassed. He wouldn't look at me.

"I'm gonna call my buddy back," he said. "See if he saw anything at my place." He then stepped out to use the pay phone again.

I stayed there on the bed, all fired up and frustrated. "F--k!" I chanted to myself, the word both a war cry and a lament.

Five minutes later Ricky returned to the room looking distraught.

"Cops are swarming all over my place," he said.

"Oh no" I responded. "What are we going to do?"

Ricky shook his head and shrugged. "They're gonna find your dad's car, find your dad. They'll trace it back to me eventually. Lock me up for good this time."

"There must be something we can do."

Ricky sighed, surrendering himself to his fate. "I'm done Verona. Might as well turn myself in. Or put a bullet in my brain."

"Don't say that Ricky!"

"What choice do I have? I'm not gonna run the rest of my life, always checking over my shoulder."

"I can't lose you! Not now!" I bawled, wringing my clothes. "I bet if you hire a great lawyer, he could get you off."

"Only someone like you gets off on stuff like this," Ricky said.

"What do you mean?" I asked him.

Ricky's eyes lit up. He had an idea for a role I knew I could play flawlessly. I was young enough he said, and I could act like I was emotionally traumatized and say it was an accident, which it was. At worst they would throw me in juvee jail until I was 21. I could save Ricky! But

"What about us?" I asked.

He gazed fiercely into my eyes and said "I can wait if you can."

"You really mean it?"

"Verona, you love me don't you?"

Yes I said. A million times yes!

"I love you too. And I don't want to lose you either. I'm thinking all this happened because it was meant to happen. Because we were meant to be together."

YES WE ARE!!!

"I believe in you" he said. "I believe in us."

Then Ricky kissed me, passionately, powerfully. His lips were warm and soft and delicate. Yet they shot me full of crashing surf and erupting volcanoes and lightning bolts. I swooned. He held me up.

When it was over I was no longer myself. Ricky became part of me. I belonged to him body heart & soul. I would do anything for him.

"You have to help me help us," he said. "Or else there'll never be an us. If I go to prison, you'll never see me again. Never touch me again. I don't want that. Do you want that?"

"No" I of course answered. I tried to mentally add up how many days it was until I turned 21 and calculated it to be Too Many. But mine would be the lesser sacrifice for the greater good.

"It's only 6 years, right?"

"Tops" Ricky said. "Then we'll be free to do whatever we want. Go wherever we want. Nothing tying us down."

"Our love tying us together!"

"You bet baby."

I wanted to kiss him again but he was already off plotting our future.

Ricky & I hatched a bold and brilliant plan. We worked superbly as a team, as partners in crime like Bonnie & Clyde. But the only thing we stole was each other's hearts!

Who would have thought how excited I would be to get arrested??

A major part of our plan depended on us getting an accomplice. Nobody would believe I had acted alone. Ricky asked if I knew anyone I trusted enough to help me and not flake out. I told him yes I did. Ricky gave me a pocketful of coins and I went out to the pay phone. I didn't know Howie's number so I had to dial information. Fortunately his family were the only Gutermuths in Merrick.

Howie's mother answered on the third ring. I asked to speak to Howie. She asked me who I was. I told her my full name and that I was a classmate of Howie's. At first his mother sounded shocked a girl was calling her son, then probably assumed I was just interested in a homework assignment or test we both had.

"Hi Howie" I said when he got on the phone.

"Verona? Hey w-w-what's up?"

"I must see you" I said dramatically. "Right now."

"Are you OK?"

"No I'm not" I croaked, pretending to snivel. "I need your help."

And that was all it took for Howie to agree to come pick me up from the motel.

After I hung up I returned to the room. Ricky was ready to go. He looked so sad. I of course didn't want him to leave either and I considered insisting we run off together that very instant but I had to respect what Ricky wanted.

Ricky asked how it went with my friend. I told him Howie wouldn't be a problem. Ricky then tenderly clasped my hands and stared intensely into my eyes.

"Your story must be surefire Verona," he said. "If they sense anything doesn't add up they'll come after me."

"Don't worry" I assured him. "I'll be perfect."

"You have to be. Or it'll all be over."

"They won't suspect you, my darling. I'll make certain of that."

"I won't forget this" Ricky said, squeezing my hands almost enough to hurt. "I owe you."

"Another foot rub?"

He smiled at me. "When you get out, all the foot rubs you want. And much much more."

Then Ricky leaned in and kissed me. I briefly shut my eyes during it but then re-opened them. I needed to remember this moment, his face so close to mine. The stubble on his cheeks, the tiny scar on the bridge of his nose, his almond shaped eyes, his deep furrowed brow. I needed to fix his image in my mind, to preserve it there for the next few years, until I could relive us for real once again.

And then our kiss was over. I could've cried.

"I better jet" Ricky said. "Your friend should be here soon."

We embraced. I didn't want to ever let him go! We were meant to be like this. To be apart seemed so wrong. But I reminded myself this wasn't the end. It was the beginning of our life together!

Ricky put on his baseball cap and opened the door.

"I love you" I said.

"You too" he said and left.

I dashed to the window and watched Ricky hurry down the road until he was gone. It felt weird seeing my Happily Ever After walking away from me. I never felt more lonely.

Dear fans, what happened next is difficult to write about but I promised I would tell my whole story, warts and all. I only pray you don't judge me too harshly. What I did I had done for true love. For Ricky.

I sat outside the motel on the curb anxiously waiting for Howie to show up.

While I was pretty confident he would go along with our plan, it wasn't quite as guaranteed as I had made it out to be. Howie was smitten with me yes, but who knew the limits of that? I would definitely be testing those limits.

45 minutes after I called him Howie cruised up in his father's Corolla. I got in and we sped off. We drove to Jones Beach. On the way I explained to Howie what had happened (as Ricky & I reimagined it) and what role I required him to play.

We parked in one of the beach's larger parking fields, by a cluster of pine trees far away from any other cars. Howie just sat there and didn't say anything for a long while, even when I chattered about less dire subjects like movies and school. His silence made me nervous.

"I can't believe you killed your dad," he finally said.

It was an accident I reiterated.

"Can't you just tell the p-p-police that?"

"It's too late now. I was really scared so I tried to make it all go away. And I only made things worse."

"And now you want me to turn myself in for s-s-something I had n-n-nothin' to do with?"

"I know it's a huge favor."

"Uh huh yeah. Monumental." Howie shook his head in bogglement. "Why do you need me for this?"

"You'll back up my story," I repeated. "So the cops won't have any reason to doubt it."

"Why w-w-would they?"

"I didn't drive my father's car into the lake by myself. Or carry his body out and put it in the trunk... My uncle was there too."

"Your uncle?"

"I was hysterical after it happened so I called him to help me. I didn't know what else to do. But he has a criminal record. If the cops learn he was involved they'll lock him up for life. He doesn't deserve that."

"But I do?"

"You're under 18 and you didn't actually kill anyone. You'd just be an accomplice. You'll do hardly any time at all!"

"But why me? I thought y-y-you didn't even like m-me?"

I had him on my leash, now I had to get him to roll over for me.

"I do like you Howie. A lot." I choked up like Ingrid Bergman in <u>Casablanca</u>. "I've been such a fool. All this time I've been searching for my perfect man. And here you were all along."

"I was?"

"I thought I wanted some dapper older gentleman with a big house and a fancy car. But now I realize I want someone who understands me. Who loves me for who I am. Who wants only me." I stroked Howie's cheek and gave him my most heartfelt smile. "I want you Howie Gutermuth."

"B-b-but you're kinda asking for a lot."

"Please Howie. You're the only one I can trust."

Howie averted his eyes from mine. "If we both go to jail," he mused "we wouldn't s-s-see each other for a long time. H-h-how do I know you'd wait for me?"

"Oh I will darling! I will!"

Howie fell mute again. I could tell he was still torn. I needed to seal the deal. I caressed his arm then his thigh. "Please Howie" I implored once more.

He pulled away from me. "No. I can't do it."

Fear and doubt were eclipsing Howie's desire for me. What could I do? I was flirting for Ricky's life — for our life! — but flirting wasn't enough. I had to go farther. I had to make another sacrifice. I had no choice!

"Let me prove it to you" I said.

I reclined my seat into a laying position. Then I hiked up my skirt and slipped off my underwear, letting it drop to my ankles.

Howie's eyes bulged as he drank in my nakedness.

"You like what you see?" I asked.

He nodded, gulped.

"Do you want me?"

He nodded again, practically drooling.

"Be gentle" I told him. "It's my first time."

It was.

Howie climbed across the seat and on top of me. While he ogled me up & down he unzipped those ugly brown corduroy pants he always wore and yanked them to his knees. He spit into his hand and touched himself, his eyes glued on me. Then he slid into me.

"Is this OK?" he asked.

"Yeah" I answered. "Feels nice."

Actually, once the feeling like I had to pee waned, I felt nothing at all. My mind had gone elsewhere. I was with Ricky on our wedding day in a spectacular gothic cathedral. He was dressed in a dashing black tux, me in a dazzling white gown. There were beautiful flowers and lit candles everywhere. Little birdies and butterflies flitted about us. We were kissing, as husband & wife, the universe spinning around us, our love burning bright as the sun.

I heard Howie in the distance say something about pulling out but then the church bells tolled and the pipe organ swelled, drowning him out.

And then it was over. The next thing I remember was Howie fetching napkins from the glovebox to clean himself off. He re-did his pants and clumsily twistered back into the driver's seat.

I felt a tad raw down there, nothing that wouldn't go away in a day or two. It would be like it never happened.

Howie grinned at me.

"I love you" he said.

I knew my puppy would now obey my every command.

An hour later we arrived at the police station. We walked in holding hands. I had to contain my enthusiasm lest Howie think something was amiss. He was clearly on edge yet I could tell he was ready to take the rap for a crime he'd taken no part in. What love will make one do.

I did feel a trifle bad about misleading him. But he wouldn't be in too much trouble, and honestly he owed me. I'm sure he'll get over me eventually.

We approached the main desk and spoke to an officer with a thick mustache. I put on my most anguished face and told him we'd like to report an accidental killing. Manslaughter they call it in legal language.

A few minutes later Howie & I were seated at a metal table in a small windowless room. An interrogation room I guess it was. A detective came in with a notepad and sat down at the table opposite us. He introduced himself as Detective Hayes. He was maybe in his 40s, Irish looking with a rugged complexion. He reminded me of John Garfield.

"OK Miss Cassidy" he said after I had rattled off a summary of my story, "Starting from when you left your house, tell me step by step what happened."

I told him after I lied to my mom about sleeping with her boyfriend, she called my father. That's when I ran off and bumped into Howie outside the Baskin Robbins. I asked him to give me a ride to my dad's house in Westchester so I could explain everything to him myself because my mom is prone to blowing stuff out of proportion. When we got to my dad's I went in and Howie stayed in the car. I found dad upstairs in his bedroom. He was loading his gun — yes a pistol — he kept it in his sweater drawer. I asked him what he was planning to do. He said he had matters to discuss with Rick. Matters that involve a gun? I said. He didn't answer. He looked so angry. He said out of my way V! and pushed past me. I chased after him. I knew he was going to hurt my mom's boyfriend. Or kill him. He was raving mad. I stopped him at the top of the stairs. I begged him not to go, told him that it was all a misunderstanding. But he wouldn't listen. I grabbed his arm. Then he slapped me and

I shoved him and he fell backward down the stairs. That's how he broke his neck.

I then unloosed the waterworks for Detective Hayes. He passed me a box of tissues.

"So I freaked out," I continued while dabbing my eyes. I was petrified I would be thrown in jail where I'd be raped or beaten or stabbed. So I convinced my boy friend Howie to help me make it all go away. I put my father's gun back in its drawer then Howie & I wrapped dad up in a bedsheet and carried him out. We drove to Lake Ronkonkoma. That's where we got rid of my dad's car. And my dad.

"You placed your father's body in the trunk of his car, correct?" asked Detective Hayes.

I nodded and blotted my eyes some more.

Detective Hayes turned his attention to Howie. "Is that how it happened son?"

"Yeah" Howie answered. "Exactly."

"So why own up to it now?" Detective Hayes asked me.

"Because it's tearing me apart!!" I cried. "I need to live with this, to face the consequences, if I'm going to live with myself." Then I improvised a bit: "I wish it was all just a terrible dream. But I'm not waking up from this." Then I whipped my head to & fro and shrieked "NOT EVER EVER EVER EVER!" and slumped forward in my chair, harrowed and haunted by my misdeeds.

Dear fans, my performance could've won me an Oscar!

Late that afternoon Detective Hayes personally drove us to Lake Ronkonkoma so I could show him the spot where we dumped my father's car. Its rear fender was still sticking out of the water. Detective Hayes radioed for other policemen to join us, including one who was a scuba diver. They hooked a chain from a tow truck to the car's fender and hauled it out.

Howie & I were standing several feet away so we couldn't really see inside the trunk when they opened it. They obviously found my father because then they formally arrested us and read us our rights.

Detective Hayes tried to cuff Howie first. That's when he snapped. He jerked his hand away and shouted "No! I didn't do anything!"

"We have to cuff you son," Detective Hayes said. "It's procedure."

"I lied!" Howie admitted. "I wasn't there!"

"What are you doing Howie?" I growled through gritted teeth.

"It was this other guy. Rick. I saw them."

How did he know that? I wondered. He couldn't know that!

"Who's Rick?" Detective Hayes asked.

"Shut the hell up Howie."

"I followed you there Verona. To Rick's p-p-place. I saw him c-c-carry your dad out."

Shit. Shit Shit Shit!

I glared at the stupid boy. "Shut. Up."

"I'm sorry" he whimpered to me. "I don't want to g-g-go to jail. I just wanted to b-be your boyfriend f-f-for a little while."

Arrrgh! Best laid plans crumble when on top of a rotten floor. And to think I let him pierce my maidenhead! I shudder thinking about it.

I was to say the very least livid. "You're ruining everything! I hate you!!!"

Howie, shamed, wouldn't look at me.

"I don't know what's going on here," said Detective Hayes, "but we're gonna iron it out at the station"

Oh no we wouldn't! I needed to warn Ricky that our plan had gone awry, that he was in jeopardy. I decided to make a break for it. I bolted for the dirt road that led us there. A policeman tackled me from behind, knocking me down and pinning me to the ground. I fought him with every ounce of resolve I had, flailing my arms and legs, kicking and punching and biting whatever I could.

I could hear the other cops laughing.

"She's a scrappy one, ain't she Ronny?"

"Careful Ronny, the kid might know karate!"

"Maybe you should call for backup Ronny!"

Ha Ha. Those bastards were cracking jokes at my expense. (and Ronny's too, I suppose)

"Let me go!" I screamed. "You're hurting me!" Ronny was pressing his full weight down on me and I was having a tough time breathing.

"Stop!" I heard Howie yell. "You're hurting her!"

I managed to scratch Ronny's cheek. He yelped. I had drawn blood. But he was undaunted.

"You b---h" the brute spat.

"Enough" Detective Hayes said. "Jim help get her under control. Pepper her if you have to."

I spotted another officer heading toward me wielding a little black aerosol can. I thrashed harder. I knew if I didn't escape now I wouldn't be able to when I'm blinded with 2 cops ganging up on me. Yet this seemed inevitable. It looked like my final scene had been written.

Then Fate, recognizing this to be quite an undignified way for me to exit the stage, demanded a re-write!

Howie somehow snatched a gun from one of the officers holsters. He aimed it at the one with the pepper spray and barked "Stay away from her!"

Everybody froze. "What do you think you're doing son?" Detective Hayes asked.

Howie didn't respond to him. "You get off of her!" he ordered Ronny, who was still on top of me but was no longer tussling with me.

"You best give that pistol back to Officer Hobbs," Detective Hayes said, "or you're gonna be in a mess more trouble than you already are."

"I don't care" Howie answered. Then to Ronny again, "I said get off her. Now!"

Ronny did.

"C'mon let me have my gun kid," pleaded Officer Hobbs, taking a cautious step toward him.

Howie fired the gun into the ground, nowhere near the policemen but he got his point across nonetheless.

"Go Verona!" Howie shouted at me as he held them at bay.

Howie my hero. My fickle and foolish hero. Undoubtedly he'd now be facing a slew of more serious charges. But his rash act would change nothing between us. Or maybe he did it for himself, to ease his guilt over ratting out Ricky & me. Whatever it was, it allowed me the opportunity to reunite with my beloved! I sprang to my feet and fled.

I ran to the same dark road Ricky & I had travelled to the motel. I had no idea how long Howie could stall the police. Even with my head start they would likely catch up with me well before I reached the first town line.

I was already winded, my legs wilting. I couldn't go on much farther without collapsing from exhaustion. Worst of all my hope was withering. Soon Ricky & I would be torn asunder, our destiny shattered, our love scattered into dust. A dreadful ending!

It was then I heard the putter of a small motor. I spotted a single headlight approaching on the road ahead. I leapt in front of it, frantically waving my arms for it to stop.

It was a bearded man on a green scooter (not unlike the one in Roman Holiday — talk about a good omen!) Instead of slowing down he veered sharply to the left, narrowly missing me. He struck a ditch on the shoulder, launching himself over the handlebars and tumbling onto the ground.

He laid sprawled on the grass. I hurried over to him. By the time I got there he was sitting up and removing his helmet.

"Oh my god, are you alright?" I asked.

"I think so" he said. "Might've tweaked my ankle though." He tried to wiggle his foot and winced. "Yeah. Don't think I'm gonna be able to walk on it. Could you"

Before he could finish his request I hopped onto his scooter and zoomed off.

"Hey!" I heard him yell behind me.

Desperate times call for desperate measures and this was an emergency! I raced down the roads, dodging traffic, beeping at pedestrians, blowing stop signs and red lights. I was on a rescue mission. I could hear you, dear fans, cheering me on. Go Verona Go!

When I arrived at Ricky's everything appeared quiet. There were no cop cars outside his building. I didn't see Ricky's Mustang either.

I got inside again courtesy of an exiting neighbor. I flew up the stairs to Ricky's floor. When I reached his door I was rather surprised there was no yellow crime scene tape covering it. I knocked. Nobody answered. I tried the knob. It was un-locked. I went in.

I knew at once something wasn't kosher. After turning on the light switch I saw the painting of the nude black lady was gone. All of Ricky's pictures and baseball items were gone. The walls were bare.

Yet all his furniture remained as they had been the last time I was there. Well, almost all. His lamps were missing too. As was his TV, his coffee maker, his ashtray. Most of his drawers and cabinets were empty. And he had taken all of his clothes and linens with him.

Ricky in haste had quit his apartment, permanently it seemed. I sought out a note he might have left for me explaining his course of action but there wasn't any. Perhaps he'd mail it to me while I was in jail and he was on the move. That would be the wise thing to do.

I sat down in Ricky's armchair and waited. Within minutes police lights swirled outside the windows. They wouldn't find Ricky but I was ready for them.

Our plan, like our love, was still alive!

Since I expressed an acceptable degree of remorse I received only 2 to 3 years in the Nassau County Juvenile Corrections Center. It's not bad. They serve us three meals a day, there's a rec room with a TV and exercise equipment, and I share a room with this latino girl Sonia who's really funny even though she cusses a lot. We have access to phones, books, and magazines too.

I couldn't go to my father's funeral though I suppose it would've been awkward if I did. I heard it was a nice, well attended affair. Somebody I never met delivered the eulogy. I recited my own for him here. I hope he liked it.

My mother visits me at least three times a week. She used to cry whenever she came but she's much better now that she's on new medication. She told me Howie got the maximum length sentence for a youthful offender. He probably wouldn't be released until his 21st birthday, which sucks for him but he would've been better off if he had just followed the plan. Mom also tells me about all the men she's dating. I don't mind listening to it. None of them are Ricky.

I haven't gotten any word from him yet. But I must be patient. Once he feels safe I know he'll contact me, tell me he'll be here when I get out. Maybe he'll whisk me away to some cabin hideaway high in the mountains where nobody can find us. There we'll snuggle up drinking hot chocolate by a stone fireplace on cold wintry nights. It'll be so romantic.

I know my fans will think ours is the greatest love story ever told, worthy of a Major Motion Picture. I wonder what actors would portray us? All the best ones are too old or dead. Maybe Ricky & I can play our selves. Then we can watch ourselves re-enacting our own story. How surreal would that be! Verona Cassidy and Ricky Fahling starring in...

A STREET CALLED DESTINY

They'll give us glowing reviews and Academy Awards. They'll put our names together on the Hollywood Walk Of Fame.

We will be legends. Our love will be immortalized.

We're going to be a classic my darling!

VC ♥ RF FOREVER   VC ♥ RF FOREVER

VC ♥ RF FOREVER   VC ♥ RF FOREVER

VC ♥ RF FOREVER   VC ♥ RF FOREVER   VC ♥ RF FOREVER

VC ♥ RF FOREVER   VC ♥ RF FOREVER   VC ♥ RF FOREVER

VC ♥ RF FOREVER   VC ♥ RF FOREVER   VC ♥ RF FOREVER

VC ♥ RF FOREVER   VC ♥ RF FOREVER   VC ♥ RF FOREVER

VC ♥ RF FOREVER   VC ♥ RF FOREVER   VC ♥ RF FOREVER

VC ♥ RF FOREVER   VC ♥ RF FOREVER   VC ♥ RF FOREVER

VC ♥ RF FOREVER   VC ♥ RF FOREVER   VC ♥ RF FOREVER

VC ♥ RF FOREVER   VC ♥ RF FOREVER

VC ♥ RF FOREVER   VC ♥ RF FOREVER

VC ♥ RF FOREVER   VC ♥ RF FOREVER

VC ♥ RF FOREVER   VC ♥ RF FOREVER

VC ♥ RF FOREVER

VC ♥ RF

FOREVER

[[END OF DOCUMENT]]

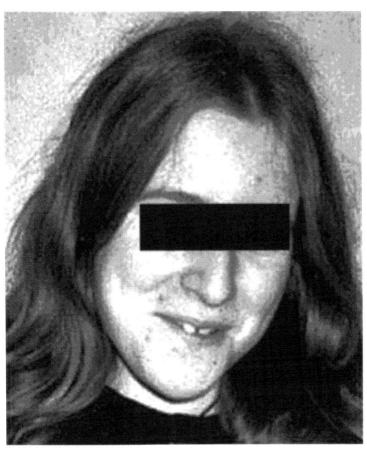

mugshot (photocopy) of Verona Cassidy
taken 5-4-86 at NCPD Seventh Precinct

AFTERWORD

Verona Cassidy was released from the Nassau County Juvenile Corrections Center on November 12, 1989, a few days after she had turned 19. She moved back into her mother's home, residing there until March 1990, when she left with a packed travel bag. She did not share details of her intended destination(s) with anyone, only telling her mother, cryptically, that she was going to get herself a "slice of moon." Verona never returned.

Her current whereabouts are unknown.

ABOUT THE AUTHOR

Sawney Hatton is an author, editor, and screenwriter. His books include the Dark Comedy novel **Dead Size** and the Dark Fiction short story collection **Everyone Is a Moon**. He also edited the Sci-Fi Horror anthology **What Has Two Heads, Ten Eyes, and Terrifying Table Manners?**

Uglyville is his first True Crime novella.

Visit the author's website at
www.SawneyHatton.com

The Publisher would like to express its gratitude to the following individuals who have contributed to this book:

Dr. Paul J. Patterson and the Graduate Writing Studies Program faculty at Saint Joseph's University; Dennis Capoferri, Misha Revlock, Beckie McDowell, Zach Tollen, and the rest of the magical gremlins in the West Philly Writers Group; Lauren Eveland; Russ Colchamiro; Andrew Whelan; Don Corcoran; Ryan Latini; Craig Kestel; and Amber Sharber

82992594R00106

Made in the USA
Middletown, DE
08 August 2018